This is what they've said about
THE ROSE TATTOO

Unspoken Confessions

"Ms. Roberts thrusts readers right into the action and will keep you guessing to the very end."
—Debbie Richardson,
Romantic Times

"The hunt is thrilling, the passion hot, the danger only too real."
—Laurel Gainer,
Affaire de Coeur

Unlawfully Wedded

"Clever plot twists keep the reader involved."
—*Rendezvous*

Undying Laughter

"It's even better than the first two!"
—Laurel Gainer,
Affaire de Coeur

Handsome As Sin

"Kelsey Roberts once again delivers sparkling dialogue and great touches of humor."
—Debbie Richardson,
Romantic Times

Dear Reader,

I hope you enjoy *The Tall, Dark Alibi*, which is definitely a tribute to the magic that I believe is part of falling in love. Of course, I had to include a very special twist.

Thanks to your overwhelming response to the blend of danger and desire offered in THE ROSE TATTOO series, Rose and the gang are back to keep you entertained and, hopefully, guessing. My editor, Bonnie Crisalli, has mentioned that my heroine, Kendall, is "classic Kelsey," which I hope means she's a strong, independent, sharp-tongued lady who certainly meets her match in Jonas Revell. I strive to make the interplay between the hero and heroine as gripping as the mystery—I want their chemistry to be as thrilling for you as the dangerous situation they face together.

And I'm not out of ideas yet, so there will be more Rose Tattoo books coming your way. At the end of this book you'll find a sneak peek at the next book in the series—*The Silent Groom*, coming in March 1997.

All the best,

Kelsey Roberts

Kelsey Roberts
The Tall, Dark Alibi

Harlequin Books

TORONTO • NEW YORK • LONDON
AMSTERDAM • PARIS • SYDNEY • HAMBURG
STOCKHOLM • ATHENS • TOKYO • MILAN
MADRID • WARSAW • BUDAPEST • AUCKLAND

For my mother, who gave me my love of history,
and my father, who always sat with me until
Dorothy clicked her heels three times.

ISBN 0-373-22395-1

THE TALL, DARK ALIBI

Copyright © 1996 by Rhonda Harding Pollero

CAST OF CHARACTERS

Dr. Kendall Butler—She travels back to 1861 and ends up a mail-order bride. Harvard Medical School didn't prepare her for this.

Jonas Revell—1861 spy. Tall, dark, handsome... and accused of killing his first wife.

Harris Grisom—He's determined to make Jonas pay for the death of his daughter. Perhaps killing Kendall is the best revenge of all.

Franklin Monroe—He's so convinced Jonas is guilty, he'll do anything to see him punished, so long as he can keep his own secrets.

Caroline Grisom—She was the only other person in the house when her sister died. How far can sibling rivalry go?

Maitland—He's got his hand in everything—possibly Cecelia's murder, as well.

William Whitefield—He's devoted to The Cause, but his motives are certainly his own.

Rose Porter—She trades her spandex and animal prints for corsets and ostrich feathers to help Kendall on her journey.

Dylan Tanner—He's an effective lawman in the present; in the past, he's even better.

Shelby Hunnicutt Tanner—Living in the midst of war hasn't changed her one bit.

Prologue

Jonas Revell climbed the stairs at a slow, deliberate pace. His footsteps echoed through the darkened interior of his new home on East Bay. Just thinking of the house and its purpose brought a dark scowl to his face. Damn, but he hated what he was about to do, what he had already done.

The chimes from the hall clock signaled the late hour. It felt much like a curse this night. How Jonas wished he had stayed in England, or perhaps settled someplace other than Charleston, as his father had suggested. Either of those options would have saved him from the task at hand, he thought with a dejected sigh.

His mind produced vivid images of the evening past. Images of Cecelia in her ornate, white gown and hand-embellished veil. The beautiful Cecelia Grisom had made an expectedly beautiful bride. Her wide eyes had followed him quietly throughout the long, nerve-racking day. Yes, she was a beautiful bride. His *bride*.

Jonas hesitated on the landing, mustering the strength for the difficult task awaiting him. His proud heritage, as well as his sense of duty, urged him on. The British portion of his genealogy insisted that he seal his pact with the Grisom family. Yet the seeds planted by his half-Navajo mother made him lament the loss of his free will.

That same sense of duty had been the driving force behind the construction of this home and the commissioning of the locket. Taking in a breath, he recalled the look in Cecelia's eyes when he'd slipped the necklace around her throat. His brow furrowed. Cecelia had shown no emotion, and though he was quite accustomed to his wife's lack of response, it had punctuated their association. With just a small dose of conceit, Jonas pondered her reaction. Or, more accurately, her lack thereof. He prided himself on his rather well-deserved reputation with the women of Charleston. He shied from utilizing the description of "lady" in reference to his companions, since he had a strict policy against pursuing the tittering, manipulative young women so common in Charleston society.

Cecelia's reaction to Jonas was something that had caused him some measure of curiosity during their brief courtship. She showed absolutely no interest in him. Her eyes followed him, but there was a distance in her gaze.

Jonas stiffened. He couldn't help but wonder if her guarded expression was because she *knew*. Or maybe she simply sensed. His fingers reached out and gripped the knob to the bedroom door. He hesitated again, hating what he was about to do, what he had to do. There was no alternative, no other option.

A few seconds later, Cecelia's final scream reverberated through the house.

Chapter One

"He's the last one," Kendall said as she pulled a sheet over the corpse.

"Finally," Joan, her technician, said with a sigh.

Snapping the latex gloves from her hands, Kendall rolled her head around on her shoulders, battling the fatigue of a thirty-six-hour shift.

"I'm going to sleep for two days," Joan said.

"You don't have two days off," Kendall reminded her as they left the morgue and its stale, chemical-heavy air.

Joan frowned, squishing the features of her round face into a mass of wrinkles. "I hate this job."

"No, you don't," Kendall said as they moved into the locker room. "You'll feel better after a good night's sleep."

"Thank you, Doctor. Should I expect a bill?"

Kendall smiled at the young woman. "Maybe. Want to come with me to the Rose Tattoo? Grab something to eat?" While she waited for Joan's response, she shrugged off her white lab coat, pulled her fanny pack from her locker and strapped it around her waist.

"No, thanks. Your aunt doesn't like me."

"My aunt doesn't like most people," Kendall teased. "Aunt Rose is a little rough around the edges."

"Rude is more like it," the other woman said. "She's always on my case about going back to school."

"You shouldn't have told her you wanted to be a doctor."

"Whatever," Joan grumbled. "Go on ahead. I think I'll just head home and zap something in the microwave."

A few minutes later, Kendall stepped from the bowels of the hospital into the harsh afternoon sunlight. Squinting behind her sunglasses, she took several deep breaths as she began the six-block trek to her aunt's restaurant on East Bay Street. Tourists, armed with video cameras and roughly folded maps, crammed the uneven sidewalks in the center of Charleston. The scent of flowers battled with the exhaust fumes from the slow-moving traffic.

Kendall could feel the heat of the sun through the thin fabric of her surgical scrubs. It felt good. After hours in the pathology lab, she needed sunlight, noise and a sea of living, breathing people. It helped to keep the horrors of her job in the proper perspective. She'd spent the last day and a half dealing with two coronaries, one homicide and four fatal accidents. Not exactly the stuff of which dreams are made.

On a whim, Kendall decided to cut through the Straw Market. The congested strip was something of a Charleston landmark. The block and a half of stalls held everything from prepackaged bean-soup starters to handcrafted sweet-grass baskets. Kendall smiled at the men and women who called out to her as she weaved through the crowd.

"Doctor!"

Years of conditioning stopped her in her tracks, and she quickly turned in the direction of the voice. A tall, thin man in eclectic, mismatched clothing offered a smile. His bright white teeth were a sharp contrast to his coffee-colored skin.

"Mr. Hines," she acknowledged warmly. "How are you? How's your wife?"

"Still grieving," he answered. There was a flash of sadness in his dark eyes before his gracious smile fell back into place. "I have something for you," he began excitedly, as he motioned her closer to his display case.

Mr. Hines and his family had been working the Straw Market for generations. His wife sold a very popular thirteen-bean soup package and gave weaving lessons to the tourists. Mr. Hines sold antique and estate jewelry.

"I thought of you when I saw this," he said as he presented her with a delicate, oval pendant. "I was going to bring it by the hospital for you."

"I can't accept this," Kendall told him as her thumb brushed the finely carved silver.

"You told me you lost one," he argued.

"I did, but I can't accept a gift—"

"We owe you, Dr. Butler. You did right by us when no one else would listen."

"I was just doing my job," she assured him.

He shook his head violently. "They were going to arrest us. Might have, if you hadn't proved we didn't do anything to our Justin."

Kendall felt a pang of emotion when she thought of the Hineses' infant son. Her body gave an involuntary shudder. She wondered if she would ever get used to performing autopsies on children. Hopefully, they would find a cure for SIDS in her lifetime.

"Take it, Dr. Butler. Take it."

Mr. Hines wrapped her hand in his with the cool locket against her palm.

"I shouldn't," she said, hesitating.

"Please?" he said softly.

Kendall gave in to the pleading quality of his voice, and the sincerity in his misting eyes. With a small nod, she said, "Okay. Thank you. Thank you very much."

Mr. Hines grinned broadly as he slipped the pendant into a dark velvet bag and tightened the gold cord. "You take care," he called as she turned to leave.

Carrying the velvet bag in her hand, Kendall quickened her pace. Aunt Rose probably had lunch waiting. Kendall grinned when she thought of her cantankerous aunt. Rose was nothing like her brother, Raymond, Kendall's deceased father. Rose was loud, opinionated and something of an exhibitionist when it came to her clothing. Raymond Butler had been a quiet, almost sheepish man, with simple needs and modest goals. Kendall still missed her parents and their memory seemed stronger as she walked toward the Tattoo. "Probably because of the locket," she surmised.

Kendall's locket—the one she had lost—contained pictures of her mother and father. She had worn that locket as a sort of memorial to them. It was as if she could open the locket, look at their pictures and feel the love they had together. Kendall sighed. She was nearing thirty and she had yet to experience the kind of magic her parents had shared together. No lightning bolts, no fireworks. Hell, she hadn't even had a decent date recently.

"It's about time," Rose snorted as soon as Kendall pushed open the door to the historic building.

"Good to see you, too," she countered as she placed a kiss on her aunt's soft cheek.

"I worry," Rose said. "Someone has to," she added snidely.

Kendall bit her lower lip. She wouldn't rise to the bait. Instead, she followed her aunt to one of the veranda tables. She waved to Shelby, her aunt's business partner. Kendall and Shelby got along well, and Kendall loved Shelby's two small children and her attentive and gorgeous husband, Dylan.

God, she thought as she took her seat, *why am I fixating on married couples?*

"You look tired," Rose observed as she sat down, smoothing the pile of lacquered and bleached-blond hair that added a good four inches to her height.

Kendall shrugged. "I am. I'm off tomorrow, so I can catch up on some sleep."

"I thought you picked this ghoulish specialty so you wouldn't have to keep these awful hours."

"We're short staffed."

Rose made a noise. "I know that feeling. We've been through three bartenders in six months. I swear, kids these days have no work ethic."

Kendall regarded her aunt. Today she had on a skintight pair of Lycra stirrup pants in a zebra print. A small, thin white shirt was tucked into the wide black-patent-leather belt cinching her tiny waist. Zebra earrings dangled from her earlobes, bobbing and swaying as she continued to rail about her staffing problems. A strand of smaller zebras formed a necklace. It reminded Kendall of circus elephants with their tails hooked in formation.

"Have you?"

"I'm sorry," Kendall said quickly. "What did you ask?"

Rose's green eyes grew accusatory as they narrowed. "Did you get a call from Joe Don?"

"Uncle Joe?"

"Uh-huh. It seems he and the coed have separated."

Kendall was sorry to hear that her uncle's second marriage was failing. She also knew better than to offer that sentiment to her aunt. "I haven't heard from him."

A crash sounded from the far side of the room and Rose leaped to her feet, cursing under her breath. "He can pay for that china out of his next check!"

She watched as her aunt stormed through the beveled-glass doors, into the main dining area, feeling sorry for whoever it was who had dropped the dishes. Rose didn't usually rage at her employees, but if Uncle

Joe had called, there was no telling what her aunt was capable of doing.

Sipping her iced tea, Kendall enjoyed the warm breeze and the beautiful surroundings. The Rose Tattoo was a Charleston Single House, complete with a dependency in the back. The house was built at about the time Fort Sumpter gained national prominence, and Kendall felt like part of history by just being there. The dependency, which had been the slave quarters, then the outdoor kitchen for the house, had been converted to a club for the Rose Tattoo patrons.

Kendall couldn't sit on the wraparound porch without trying to imagine what the house had been like before this part of Charleston had evolved into a commercial district. Back when true gentlemen built graceful homes for their genteel, proper wives, who saw to the decor and lavish parties that so defined the pre-war South.

When it became clear that her aunt wouldn't be returning immediately, Kendall unhooked her fanny pack, reached in and pulled out the velvet bag. Carefully, she tugged on the cord and pulled out the pendant.

Rolling it in her hand, she admired the ornately worked surface. Using her fingernail, she found the catch that opened the locket. She felt her eyes widen when she saw him.

The left side of the locket was empty, but the right side held a clear, well-aged photograph of a dashingly handsome man. He had long, dark hair and his clothing suggested the midnineteenth century. *"Hell-oooo,"* she whispered as the tip of her finger traced the sharp angle of his chin. The picture was black and white, but she could tell by the contrast that his eyes were light. Blue, maybe? she thought as she continued to stare at the attractive image.

Curious, she worked the photograph free and turned it over. It had been taken in Charleston in 1861, according to the faded photographer's mark on the back of the one-inch image. But there was nothing except handwritten initials to tell her the identity of the man with the deep cleft in his chin. "J.R.," she said, reading the faded printing. "John? Joseph? James?" she suggested, turning the photo over to try the names on the handsome face. "Nope, you don't look like a John."

"Who doesn't?" Rose asked.

"Him," Kendall said as she replaced the photograph and handed Rose the opened locket.

"Cute. Too bad he's too old for you."

Kendall offered a saccharine smile. "Funny."

"What are you doing with this?"

Kendall took back the locket. "It was a gift."

"From a man?" Rose brightened.

Kendall nodded.

"Now you're getting somewhere," Rose said. "Does this man have a name?"

"Mr. Hines."

"Hines?" Rose repeated. "Wasn't he the guy who beat his kid to death?"

"He didn't beat the child," Kendall corrected firmly. "The newspaper put the real story on the back page, several days after they'd branded him a murderer on the front page."

"Oh, well, anyway, what about some of those other doctors? Why do you have such a hard time finding a man?"

"Rose?" Shelby's soft voice held a definite warning. "I hope you're not giving Kendall grief about her social life again."

Kendall smiled at the tall, elegant brunette as she floated over to their table. Shelby Hunnicutt Tanner was truly a Southern lady. She had more class in her little finger than most women had in their whole body. If she wasn't so nice, she would definitely be the kind of woman other women hated.

"What social life?" Rose grumbled. "When I was her age, I had kids already."

"Well," Shelby said, with a sigh. "I didn't, so don't be so hard on her."

"How are you?" Kendall asked.

"Cassidy is teething and Chad is a handful. Dylan has his moments, too."

Shelby's whole face glowed as she spoke of her husband and her two children. The teasing light in her blue eyes told Kendall that she was hating every minute of her daughter's teething, but was tolerant as usual. She also knew that Chad was a very loved little boy, who had both his parents wrapped around his little finger.

"Is Dylan in town?"

Shelby shook her head. "He should be back tonight."

"How come we're talking about her?" Rose griped. Leveling her eyes on Kendall, she added, "You're the one who can't seem to get a date."

"I can get dates," Kendall insisted. "I'm just not interested right now."

"That's garbage," Rose scoffed. "If you're breathing, you're interested." Rose stilled and looked stricken. "You're not…you do like guys, don't you?"

Kendall chuckled and rolled her eyes. "Yes, Aunt Rose. I'm completely heterosexual."

Rose breathed a sigh of relief.

"Not that it should matter," Kendall commented.

"I just need to know where to look," Rose explained. "There's a guy who comes in every Friday—"

"No, thanks," Kendall cut in. "I don't want to be fixed up. I've told you that."

"You don't seem to be doing much on your own," Rose argued. "I think you need a push in the right direction."

"Absolutely not."

"All you have to do is tell me the kind of man you want," Rose explained as the jukebox began playing "Love Me Tender." Elvis was the only music ever played at the Tattoo, thanks to her aunt's fixation with the King. "Tall, thin. You tell me, and I'll keep on the lookout."

"This ought to be rich," Shelby muttered.

"I'm serious," Rose bellowed. "Tell me the kind of guy you want."

Kendall closed her eyes briefly and then nodded. Flipping open the locket, she said, "I wouldn't mind him."

"He's dead."

"Then I guess you'll just have to give up on your little plan."

Rose was about to argue, when yet another crash from the kitchen echoed through the restaurant. Rose frowned as she and Shelby scurried off to assess the damage.

"Saved again," Kendall said to the handsome man's photograph. Carefully, she closed the locket and lifted the chain over her head.

She felt hot, and for a fraction of a second, she experienced a spinning sensation. When her head cleared, it was dark. "Am I dead?" She felt a cool breeze as she waited for her eyes to adjust to the dark. "Did the power go out?" She began to be aware of her surroundings, though what she found seemed impossible. "I'm outside," she gasped, feeling the cool earth beneath her palms.

Hearing the rustling of leaves, she searched the shadows for signs of life. Shock gave way to relief. Good, someone was coming, and maybe he or she could explain how she'd gotten from lunch at the Rose Tattoo to the woods in the middle of the night.

"Did I get pricked at the lab?" she wondered aloud. Maybe she was just having some sort of strange hallucination that had caused her to sleepwalk. There had to be a logical explanation.

The footsteps grew closer and Kendall pushed herself off the ground. "Rose?" she called out.

The branches of the pines danced on a strong breeze, but there was no response. The scent of a horse reached her nostrils, and she turned into a clearing, trying to listen for the footsteps. Nothing.

"Hey, you—" she called out. "Help me, please. I'm a doctor." God, she groaned inwardly, that sounded lame.

She felt something long and hard jab into her back. Reflexively, she spun, arms raised. "I'm a—"

She went silent. There was just enough moonlight for Kendall to see him. Just enough moonlight for her to know that she was looking up into a familiar face...the face of the man in the locket. And he was pointing a rather large gun right at her head.

Chapter Two

"There's no need for a weapon, pal," she stammered.

"Silence," he fairly bellowed as he lowered his gun fractionally. "Who are you?"

"Dr. Kendall—"

"The truth," he barked, returning the gun to a trajectory ominously close to her heart.

Moving her hands, palms toward the man, she swallowed and began again. Speaking in slow, measured tones, she said, "I'm Kendall Butler."

One dark brow rose toward the brim of his hat. A hat that matched his period costume. The man was huge, with broad shoulders and a tightly coiled stance that made her think of a panther about to go in for the kill. Even without the gun, he appeared fully capable of killing her with his gloved hands.

What the hell is going on? she thought as she battled the fear knotting her stomach.

"Look," she began, forcing bravado into her voice. "I don't know what I've stumbled across here."

"Like hell."

The menace behind the clipped delivery did little to assuage her anxiety. Kendall focused on his clothing, wishing there were more light. She would feel a whole lot more comfortable if she could see his expression. Even better if she had the first clue about what she was doing in the woods with a man who looked just like a guy who must have been dead for more than a century.

Slowly, ever mindful of the gun, Kendall dropped her arms to her sides. Her mind raced along with her pulse. Though she couldn't see his eyes, she could certainly *feel* them. It was like nothing she had ever experienced. The cool night air separating them seemed to heat up as he studied her.

When he finished, she could hear the frown in his voice. "I'll give you one more chance to explain yourself, Madame."

"Madame?" she repeated. "Obviously, I've wandered into something here. For that, I apologize. However, I would feel a whole hell of a lot better if you would point that gun someplace else."

"I'm sure you would," he responded smoothly, though the gun remained trained on her. "Explain yourself."

"I've been trying to," she assured him. "I was having lunch with my aunt, then somehow I ended up here, in the middle of your little production."

"Production?"

"You're one of those reenactors, right? That's the deal with the clothes and that antique gun."

"Excuse me?"

"I must have been more tired than I thought," Kendall said, more to herself than to the tall, dark man standing before her. "I must have blacked out after lunch, and my aunt is doing this as some sort of joke, right?" Kendall sighed. "Or maybe I accidentally ingested something at the lab that is causing one hell of a hallucination. But, most likely, I've stumbled onto one of your group's recreation practices. Sorry, pal."

"This incessant chatter is all very interesting, but it hardly explains your presence here."

"I'm not supposed to be here," she asserted. "I'm sure if you wander around some more, you'll find the woman who is supposed to be playing this part. Just tell me how to get out of here, or point me in the direction of the closest phone, and I'll be on my way."

He made a sound, something akin to a derisive snort. "Phone?"

"Telephone," she repeated. "I'll call a cab and—"

"There are no carriages to rent here at Fairhaven."

"Fairhaven?" Kendall paused and looked around. A plethora of live oaks and dense pines surrounded her. "There's a convenience store at the corner of Fairhaven Road and Bohicket," she explained. "I can call from there."

"And who do you think will hear your call in the middle of the night?"

"Hopefully, the state police," she mumbled.

"State police?" The man almost laughed aloud. "You're welcome to try," he said. His voice was deep, rich and more than just a little bit menacing. "But I doubt the battalions on either side would allow you to get very far. Besides, I can't allow you to—"

A loud explosion shook the earth beneath her feet, propelling her into the arms of the tall man. Dirt rained on her hair as they tumbled backward, hitting the ground with a hard thud.

"What the hell—" Kendall began, only to have her words choked off when the man wrapped one powerful arm around her waist and rolled them in one lithe movement. His full weight pushed the air from her body. Kendall tried to shove him off of her, but it wasn't even an option. Her fingers closed on his shoulders and she felt tightly corded muscles beneath her hands. The man was solid and strong—and incredibly heavy. "Please . . ." she managed to rasp.

"Revell?"

Kendall was still pushing against his rigid body when she heard the new voice. In a flash, the man atop her stood, dragging her with him in the process.

Tears stung her eyes as she sucked in deep breaths. His gloved fingers bit into the exposed flesh of her upper arms as he pulled her up.

"What is this?" the other man growled.

"A problem," her captor answered.

"This has gone far enough," Kendall said, jerking her arm in a futile attempt to break his hold. The one called Revell no longer held the gun, so she felt a tad more assertive. "I don't know what you jerks think—"

The man grabbed her around the waist, holding her painfully against him. She could feel him go rigid against her back as his other hand came up to cover her mouth. Kendall tasted leather and the renewal of her fears.

"This wasn't a smart move on your part, Revell," the newcomer warned. "Not that I'm opposed to whoring, but your... urges have cost the girl her life."

"Hold on," she heard him say.

"What manner of clothing is that?" he asked, taking a step closer. He reached forward and took a lock of Kendall's hair between his stubby finger and thumb. "Would you share her before we conclude our business?"

Kendall's eyes grew wide with genuine fright, and she tried to turn away from the offensive little man. Her effort was aided when Revell twisted her just beyond the man's grasp.

"She is my concern, Maitland."

"Hardly," the smaller, balding man insisted. "One slip of the tongue and we're both dead. And I can assure you, I have no intention of dying for a woman."

"This is my land, Maitland. I can ill afford another dead woman on my property so soon on the heels of the last."

Kendall struggled in earnest. The deadly calm of his statement inspired her to action. *These guys are nuts,* she thought as she twisted against his rock-hard body and steely grip.

"I'm afraid I cannot abide your—"

The man holding her produced another gun, a smaller version of the first. Only this time he pointed it at the man called Maitland. "I'll deal with her."

"Be reasonable," Maitland argued. "The risks to both of us are too great to leave to chance."

"I don't leave anything to chance," Revell countered. "The documents are in my saddlebag. Take them and ride out of here."

Maitland didn't move. "I arranged the cannon fire to keep suspicion from you. Now you ask me to risk everything for her?"

"I'm not asking," Revell responded in a voice that left little doubt but that he meant it.

Maitland hesitated only a minute before he dipped his head and moved out of the clearing. Kendall relaxed against his hold and waited. He must have sensed her acquiescence, for the viselike grip slackened. It was just what she had counted on.

Using all her strength, Kendall kicked his shin. The man grunted and released her. She hit the ground running. Unfortunately, she got no more than a few yards before being tackled by the huge man.

In no time, she found herself flat on her back with his weight pressing her painfully against the hard earth. She fought, fueled by the memory of his words. *Another dead woman.*

"Stop it," he said harshly.

"I don't think so," she said, just before she sank her teeth into his shoulder.

He jerked away before she did any real damage, but his hands still gripped her wrists and his weight held her immobile. "I can call Maitland back and he can finish this."

Kendall went still. "Please," she pleaded. "I don't know what this game is all about."

"Game?"

"Whatever you and your friends are doing, you're scaring me."

He lifted his massive torso, easing the pressure on her chest which allowed her to breathe more comfortably.

"I think it is you who are playing a game, Madame, a very dangerous one."

His breath washed over her face as he loomed above her. His hat had come off at some point and long, thick, dark hair now framed his angled face. Moonlight filtered through the trees, casting shadows of dancing light.

"If you'll just let me go, I'll forget this ever happened."

"I'm afraid I can't do that," he said on an expelled breath.

"Sure you can," she insisted. "You just get off of me and we each go on our merry way."

He shook his head. "Not until I know your purpose here."

"What's that supposed to mean? I already explained, I don't belong here!"

He pulled himself into a sitting position, bringing Kendall up with him. His hold on her wrists didn't falter, nor did the stern expression marring what she could now tell was a very handsome face. Even more handsome than the picture in the locket.

"The locket," she said excitedly.

"What nonsense are you speaking now?"

A smile teased the corners of her mouth. "She did this, didn't she? She put you up to this little charade."

Kendall was again dragged to her feet, and the man pulled her wrists together, holding them in one large hand.

"Your prattling is beginning to annoy me."

"Prattling?" she repeated with a half laugh. "You're good," she told him. "You could almost make me believe you're him."

A frown creased his brow as he guided her toward the trees at the edge of the clearing. "Now you wish me to believe that you've mistaken me for someone?"

"Look at the locket," she insisted. "Then you can tell me how the two of you managed this. Hey! What are you doing?"

"Tying you up," he answered smoothly.

Too smoothly.

"I think you're carrying this a bit far, don't you? I mean, the gun and the phony explosions were bad enough, but the rope is taking it over the edge."

Ignoring her, he wrapped the rough cord around her wrists. "Forgive me if I don't trust you for the ride back to town."

"Finally," she said with a sigh. "I'll be sure to tell my aunt how well you played your part. How did she find you? You look so much like him."

"Like who?" he asked, his voice slightly raised.

"The guy in the locket. Around my neck."

His eyes dropped to the delicate chain. One brow arched as he took the chain and began to ease the locket out from beneath the shirt of her surgical scrubs.

Kendall felt the warmth of his hand in spite of his leather gloves. She could feel the smooth locket sliding against her skin. But most of all, she could feel his eyes on her.

She was smiling up at him, until she saw that his expression had taken a sudden and nasty turn. While he held the locket in his palm, his other hand reached up and grabbed a handful of her hair. With a forceful tug, he yanked her head back and took a step closer.

"Ouch," she cried. "You're hurting me."

"I'll do more than that unless you tell me where you got this."

"Go to hell," she said, wondering why she was antagonizing the man. Remembering all her self-defense training over the years, Kendall quickly complied with his request. "From Mr. Hines."

"Hines?"

"A man who sells jewelry at the Straw Market."

He took another step and Kendall countered as best she could. Unfortunately, she found her back against a tree. There was no more room for retreat. This lunatic had a firm hold on her hair and the look in his eyes was purely murderous. She would kill her aunt when this was over. Rose might have told the guy to do the macho thing, but this was going too far.

"You're lying, Kendall."

The sound of her name on his lips shouldn't have mattered. But it did. It made him seem all the more threatening. This might be Rose's idea of fun, but she'd had quite enough. Before she lost her nerve, Kendall brought her knee up hard.

He grunted when she made contact. He also let go of her hair. Wasting no time, Kendall lowered her head and rammed him, knocking him to the side. He stumbled, doubled over from the injury to what she felt certain was his most prized portion of his anatomy. *Good,* she thought as she blindly ran forward, *I hope he's green.*

The bindings on her hands were awkward and affected her balance, but she pressed on, doing her best to slap the low branches away from her face. Twigs crunched beneath her feet as she ran over the uneven terrain. Weaving around the trunk of a gnarled oak, Kendall felt the sharp pain between her shoulder blades just a second before she felt the stab of pain in her head. Then she felt nothing.

IT SEEMED as if she was being shaken gently—no, rocked, she amended as she regained consciousness. She groaned and tried to roll onto her side. "What the—"

"Silence," he commanded against her ear. "I would have no difficulty killing you after what you did at Fairhaven."

"I swear you're—"

Kendall felt the arm around her midriff tighten, forcing the breath from her body.

"You will not make another sound."

She nodded, knowing he could feel the movement since her head was against his chest. Her head hurt and her ribs weren't exactly happy. She was sitting in front of him—on a horse!

"Where are—"

"You seem to have a definite problem in taking direction, Madame. You will not utter another sound."

Yep, Rose was a dead aunt when this little charade was over. Kendall now regretted telling her aunt that she was attracted to self-confident men. Apparently, Rose had confused self-confident with arrogant and nasty. Those two adjectives seemed to describe this man to a tee. It may have been a cute idea, but Rose was going to catch hell for this.

Kendall saw the lights burning up ahead. She heard the sounds of the harbor and smelled the unmistakable scent of fire and animals. Straining against his hold, she sat upright, her mouth opened in shocked dismay. It wasn't possible. It had to be a dream. It had to be a hallucination. It had to Charleston.

Raising her bound hands to her mouth, Kendall gasped. He stopped his horse in front of the house and slipped down from the animal's back. Then, apparently catching her expression, he stood still.

"I see you recognize my house."

Kendall simply stared. "It isn't possible," she whispered.

His hands wound around her waist, lifting her gently down from the saddle. It was only then that Kendall felt the weight of the cape draped over her shoulders.

"Since I couldn't find where you discarded your gown, I took pity on you and shared my cape."

"It isn't possible," she repeated, too shocked to move. "This can't be happening."

"You should have considered that before you decided to steal from me," he growled against her ear. "Come."

He grabbed the rope tying her wrists and led her up the steps as if she were some sort of animal on a leash. Kendall stared straight ahead, trying to make sense of what she was seeing and hearing.

The front door opened as they reached the threshold. An elderly man with skin the color of strong coffee ushered them inside with his eyes downcast. "Good evening, sir."

"Jeffreys," Revell acknowledged as he dragged Kendall into the house.

Again a small sound of utter disbelief rumbled in her throat.

"Have a tub brought up to the yellow room and ask Mrs. McCafferty to find a suitable gown and bring it, as well."

Kendall was pulled through the foyer, to the stairs. "Wait," she pleaded. "Please?"

His stopped, though reluctantly, turning only his head as his deep gray eyes bore down on her. He studied her face, his frown deepening in the process. "You're white as a sheet, Madame. Finally you appreciate the foolishness of your actions."

"This is the Rose Tattoo," she told him. "Only it isn't."

"This is my home," he corrected, none too gently.

"What happened to my Aunt Rose, and how did you do all this?" she asked.

She saw the flicker of recognition in his eyes. "Who is this aunt you speak of?"

"Rose," she answered. "Rose Porter."

The man let out a descriptive expletive and then bellowed for Jeffreys again. The small butler appeared almost instantly.

"Yes, sir?"

"Go to the apothecary and fetch Mrs. Porter. Tell her it is a matter of some urgency."

Lifting her bound hands, Kendall brushed her fingertips across the back of his hand. "How did you do all this?"

"All what?" he asked impatiently.

"This," she answered, waving her hands in an arc. "All the tables are gone and there are more walls, the—"

"Come," he interrupted sharply.

Kendall was taken up to the second floor and led into the storeroom. But it wasn't a storeroom. It was a bedroom. A bedroom filled with nineteenth-century furnishings. Two young boys were heating buckets of water in a huge pot near the fireplace.

"Leave us," he said.

The two young men nodded and quickly exited the room. He seemed bigger now that they were in a confined area. The scowl marring his ruggedly handsome face didn't help matters either.

"How do you know Rose?"

"Funny," she replied, unable to keep the sarcasm from her voice. "I don't know what she led you to believe about me, but you went way overboard."

"Overboard?"

Kendall glared at the big man, which was about as defiant as she could get given that her hands were still bound by the ropes. "The gun, the faked scene with that Maitland guy. But especially these," she finished, thrusting her hands forward. "I guess my aunt failed to mention that I was a surgeon. Do you have any idea what a serious injury to my hands would mean to my career?"

He was silent as several minutes passed, with him just leaning against a washstand, staring.

His scowl grew darker. "Obviously, that bump on your head has affected your capacity, Madame."

"Just untie me before my aunt shows up. Rose has a nasty temper."

"True," came a familiar sound from the doorway. "But I like to think I'm fair."

Spinning on the balls of her feet, Kendall turned to face her aunt. "Aunt Rose! Not you, too!" she wailed.

Rose stood in the doorway, clad from head to toe in some sort of chartreuse outfit complete with feathers and garish beads. A small cigarette, which looked much like a thin cigar, extended from a jeweled holder clasped between two of her gloved fingers.

"Jonas, I'm afraid your lady friend has me at a disadvantage."

Kendall looked from her aunt to the man relaxing against the window seat. His head was slightly tilted to one side, his expression mocking and much too superior for her liking.

"Enough of this garbage!" Kendall yelled. "I do not find this funny and I think you overstepped the bounds of good taste this time, Aunt Rose."

Rose grunted. "Dressed like that, I don't know if you're in a position to comment on good taste."

Her aunt and the man shared smiles.

"Fine." Kendall sighed. "But I'm outta here."

Kendall moved toward the door, but the large hand that appeared on her arm prevented her from making much progress.

"Thanks, Rose," he said, as his fingers pinched Kendall's skin. "I'll send word across the street if I need anything else."

"Looks like you've got your hands full, Jonas."

"You can't be serious, Aunt Rose. Don't you dare leave me here with this jerk!"

Rose lifted her chin and offered a sly smile. "Interesting young lady, Jonas. She doesn't seem to be taken by your charm."

"Charm?" Kendall groaned. "I don't know where you found him, but you should have been more careful. He carries a gun, he's got some low-life friends and he's taking his role a bit too seriously for my tastes. You have to stop this, Aunt Rose. Whatever drug you put in my iced tea worked. I blacked out and this charade has—"

"Quite a temper, Jonas. Good luck."

"Rose!" Kendall called as her aunt left on a swirl of silk and satin. "Let go of me!" she insisted, giving her arm a futile yank. "Fine, you've proved you're stronger than I am. I'm sure that should get you some brownie points at your health club."

"The only club I belong to has nothing to do with health," he said close to her ear.

"Save your seductive whispers and domineering personality for someone who cares, Jonas. I'm *really* getting tired of this."

"As am I, Madame."

He spun her around to face him, and in doing so, Kendall spotted the flash of movement at the window. Seeing the hand with the gun raised, she simply reacted. Unfortunately, her reaction wasn't quite fast enough.

Chapter Three

"Oh, God," Jonas moaned as she tried to roll him off of her.

"What?" a heavyset woman, flanked by the three house attendants, came into the room. "Lord Revell!"

"Hurry," Kendall instructed. "Get him off me and untie my hands."

Kendall met the woman's eyes and saw the resistance there. "Look, lady, the bullet entered through the chest wall. My guess, from the gurgling sounds he's making, is that His Lordship has a punctured lung. You can either help me, or we can all stand around while he drowns in his own blood."

"Wha-what can you do?"

"I'm a doctor," she stated flatly.

"The dickens you say."

Kendall made a short sound and Jonas groaned. "Fine, then I suggest you put him someplace comfortable. It will take hours, if not days, for the lack of oxygen to cause sufficient brain damage to affect his vital organs."

The older woman locked eyes with Kendall as she said, "Jeffreys, you men get him on the bed. Careful, now," she cautioned in a faint Irish brogue. Then she yelled downstairs for someone to fetch Mrs. Porter.

"My hands?" Kendall prompted as she got to her feet.

The woman gave a curt nod, and a moment later, Kendall's hands were finally free. She went immediately to the bed and began tearing away Jonas's bloody shirt.

"Mrs. McCafferty?" the man called Jeffreys asked.

"Help her," she agreed. "If His Lordship can be helped."

"He can," Kendall insisted as she began to examine the wound. "I'm going to need some things."

"Yes, Madame?" Jeffreys asked.

Raking her hands through her hair, Kendall said, "I can stabilize him now until the ambulance gets here. I know a good pulmonary surgeon—"

"What happened?" Rose bellowed as she came into the room and immediately went to Jonas's side, her face brimming with concern. "Did you do this?" she hissed at Kendall.

"Funny, Aunt Rose. You have to stop screwing around now. This man needs an ambulance."

Kendall ripped a portion of Jonas's shirt and wadded it in her hand before she pressed it hard against his wound. He groaned just before his head fell to the side.

"I don't know what you're talking about," Rose said. "Are you some sort of nurse or midwife?"

"Stop it, Aunt Rose!" Kendall yelled. "If we don't get this man some medical treatment soon, he'll die."

"Doc Faraday is out at the fort seeing to the men. He wouldn't come even if we could get through to him out there."

"We need to get this man to the hospital."

"The hospital is closed, Madame. It looks like I'll have to trust my instincts and let you tend to him."

"You know my name is Kendall." Her head whipped up and she gaped at her aunt. Only it wasn't her aunt, just as it wasn't the Rose Tattoo and it apparently wasn't the 1990s anymore. The only concrete reality was the man and his wound. She chose to focus on that instead of trying to figure out just what was going on.

"You own an apothecary, right?"

Rose nodded.

"Do you have ether, laudanum, some sponges, some sulfa and some silk and needles?"

"Jeffreys, go to the shop and get what she needs."

"I'll also need as many pliers, tweezers and clamps as you can get your hands on. Oh, and a scalpel or something thin and sharp."

Within an hour, Kendall had managed to create a crude, if functional, operating theater. Perspiration dotted her brow as she placed the ether-soaked cloth across Jonas's still face. "I hope I'm not overdoing it," she mumbled. The safe and effective use of ether hadn't been part of her training, so she was winging it. She did know enough to tell them all to cover their own noses and mouths to keep from breathing in the vapors.

Mrs. McCafferty, Rose, and the three other men remained in the room, each holding a candle above Jonas. "I assume you know what you're doing?" Rose asked as Kendall moved the small blade toward Jonas's body.

"Graduated third in my class," Kendall offered, meeting the woman's clear green eyes.

"Then get on with it."

Kendall spent the next four hours performing a procedure that should have taken no more than ninety minutes. The poor light, crude implements and lack of a competent assistant made it more difficult than she could have imagined. Still, by the time she knotted the last suture, she felt more like a doctor than she had in years.

"He'll sleep for a while longer," she told those gathered at his bedside. "The longer the better."

"Will he live?" The question came from Mrs. McCafferty.

"In a couple of days, he'll be up and around. In a month, he should be good as new."

"Then I believe you have earned a drink," Rose said, taking Kendall's elbow and steering her from the room.

"I'd rather go home," Kendall said, suddenly very tired.

Rose deposited her in a high-backed chair in a narrow room at the rear of the house. It should have been the kitchen. But it wasn't.

After placing an ornate crystal glass filled with amber liquid in her hand, Rose took the seat opposite her. Their eyes met in the silence.

"Drink it. You look like you could use it."

"I could use an explanation."

Rose nodded. "It could have been anyone. Jonas has a lot of enemies."

"Not the shooting. I mean all this," Kendall said. "It's as if I'm in some other time."

Rose's expression stilled. "If you keep up that talk, they'll take you to a sanitarium."

"But it's true," Kendall cried. "Look at me. Do I look like one of you?"

"The clothes are a tad unusual, but I must admit, I was impressed by your skill and knowledge. Were you trained in the north?"

"Harvard," she answered automatically. Annoyance caused her to frown when she heard Rose's snort of disbelief. "You watched what I did upstairs. Do you think I learned that on the back of a turnip truck?"

"Truck?"

Kendall groaned. "What day is it?"

"November 19."

"What year?"

Rose's brows drew together as she answered, "Eighteen sixty-one."

Kendall started laughing. "This is rich. This is the most realistic dream I've ever had. I just wish I would wake up."

"You're fully awake," Rose insisted. "And in great danger."

"Danger?"

Rose took a sip from her drink. "It isn't exactly healthy to associate with Jonas Revell."

"Why? Why did someone try to shoot him?"

"If that's what they were about."

"I don't like the sound of that, Aunt Rose."

"Why do you do that?"

"What?"

"Insist on calling me your aunt. We are no relation. My only brother is dead."

"Raymond?" Kendall countered, getting some measure of satisfaction at Rose's shock.

"How is it you know the name of my brother?"

"He's my father," Kendall answered, feeling quite smug at having the upper hand. It didn't last long.

"That isn't possible." Rose got to her feet, walked to the fireplace and pulled on an ornate rope. "I see my friend Jonas was warranted in his suspicions of you."

"You know I'm telling the truth."

"Hardly," Rose replied, a definite chill in her green eyes. Jeffreys appeared then, with the two other housemen close on his heels. "Lock her in the bedroom until Jonas determines how to best deal with her."

"Aunt Rose?" Kendall cried.

"You should have planned your deceit more carefully, my dear."

"I'm telling the truth!"

"My brother died in a riding accident."

"I know."

"He was only five. A sight young to be siring children."

JONAS ROLLED CAREFULLY, testing his body, his hand still holding the small note recently delivered by Jeffries. He read it again, somehow hoping that he had misunderstood. He hadn't. Rose was nothing if not precise. He needed a plan.

Hoisting himself up onto the edge of the bed, he felt his brows furrow as he tried to concentrate. But Kendall and her persistent ramblings about being from another time kept creeping into his thoughts. He took a second to burn the small piece of paper, tossing it into the fireplace at the last second.

The smell of smoke filled his nostrils. "It is a preposterous notion," he grumbled as he stroked his chin. Yet he could so easily recall the look of total shock on her face when she'd walked through his home.

He also recalled how she had described the small attic. "How could she know that?" he wondered aloud. Then there was her odd clothing. No, odd wasn't quite strong enough. He rose, moved to his wardrobe and opened the doors, then pulled the bottom drawer.

As he lifted her shirt and pants, his eyes fell to the locket, and he took that out, as well. Jonas carried the items to his bed, carefully laying them out for closer inspection. Perhaps she was a spy. Perhaps all her strange ramblings were nothing more than a ploy to make certain he'd think her daft. If she knew so much about him, then certainly she would realize he wouldn't turn her over to the authorities if she was short of sense.

That thought brought a wry smile to his lips. From what little he knew of her, and from the reports he'd been getting from his staff, Kendall Butler wasn't short on anything. It seemed that she had won them over by saving his life.

Shaking his head, Jonas tried again to focus. The woman seemed a contradiction at every turn. When she had been brought appropriate clothing, she had acted as if she had never before seen a corset. Yet she had removed a bullet from his chest that, by all accounts, should have left him dead. He felt nothing but a slight twinge of pain if he took a deep breath. It was remarkable. As remarkable as Kendall, he thought as he closed his eyes and summoned her image for a second.

Jonas returned his attention to the clothing. The fabric was thin and soft, and some sort of insignia was stamped on the back, though he didn't recognize the symbol or the letters.

"So how did she get this?" he asked himself as he picked up the locket and turned it once in his palm before opening it. "And what has she done with Cecelia's picture?"

Closing the locket, Jonas frowned. This was getting him nowhere; at least, not if Rose's warning was to be taken seriously. And he knew it was.

Stuffing the strange clothing back into his wardrobe, Jonas found a special hiding place for the locket, since he knew Kendall was insisting on its return—some nonsense about believing it could send her home.

He dressed, though his mind remained fixed on thoughts of the woman in the room across the hall. He had gone in there only twice in the past week, both times in the early hours of the morning. Both times she had been asleep. Both times she had looked beautiful, peaceful.

Sighing, Jonas buttoned his shirt and set his mind to work. If he didn't think of something quickly, Kendall and her strange ramblings would no longer be his concern. She would be dead.

TWO WEEKS PASSED. Two long, boring, confining, infuriating weeks. Kendall had been transformed in that time. Outwardly. She was a mess on the inside. The dream had turned into a nightmare. A very lonely one.

"How can Rose be Rose and yet not Rose?" Kendall asked as she went to the window and stared without seeing. "How can she look the same and talk the same and not be Rose?"

Kendall gazed down at herself and smiled without humor. "How can I be standing in the Rose Tattoo dressed like Scarlett O'Hara?" How could *this* Rose have a brother who died in childhood? "How can there be two Roses?"

Kendall let out a long breath as she rubbed her temples. Her head actually hurt from trying to understand what was happening to her. She began to pace, trying to think of a rational explanation. None came.

"There cannot be two Roses and people cannot travel through time," she proclaimed to the empty room. Stopping in front of the mirror above the dry sink, she asked her reflection, "Really? Then why have you been locked in this room for two weeks? And how do you explain the fact that Charleston is littered with horses and has no bathrooms?"

Kendall returned to her pacing.

Mrs. McCafferty had told her that Jonas had recovered from his wounds, but she had yet to see the man. "Not even a friggin' thank-you," Kendall grumbled as she stood next to the fire.

When the door opened, she didn't even turn. She didn't have to. It was almost eight o'clock, which meant Jeffreys had her dinner tray. "I'm not hungry."

"Pity."

Kendall whirled around and found Jonas framed in the doorway. His eyes slid over her with amazing intimacy. Kendall decided it bothered her only because of her weeks of deprivation. That was the only explanation for her racing pulse. Her imprisonment had left her starved for companionship.

"You're looking well," she offered flatly.

Something passed in his eyes, a flash of recognition, something that apparently he preferred to keep to himself.

"I'm back to my normal constitution."

"Does that mean I can leave now?"

He crossed his arms over his broad chest and hooked one booted ankle over the other. He looked relaxed and confident, which was more than Kendall could say about herself.

"I'm afraid I can't allow that just yet. Not until I know how you came to have my wife's locket."

The fact that "wife" came out sounding like a curse wasn't lost on Kendall. Thanks to Rose and Mrs. McCafferty, she knew all about Jonas and his one-day marriage to Cecelia Grisom. She even knew that he had only married the woman to get access to her father's wharf. And, if she believed the gossip, he'd killed her on their wedding night.

"It was a gift," she said.

His dismissive nod irked her.

"Come."

"Go to hell."

"I have been informed that your... vocabulary is quite explicit. Not very ladylike, Madame."

"Madame" sounded as much like a curse as "wife."

"Ladylike doesn't interest me, Jonas. I prefer to think of myself as a woman. An intelligent, independent woman."

His smile very nearly took her breath away. She reminded herself that he probably wielded that smile like a weapon. Still, the display of even white teeth and that incredible dimple at the corner of his firm mouth was almost more than her attention-deprived senses could handle.

"That explains why Rose has taken such an interest in your well-being."

"You're wrong. Rose hasn't spoken to me since the night you were shot."

"But she's spoken with me," he informed her. "Now, would you care to join me for dinner?"

"Join you?"

He shrugged. The action caused his white linen shirt to mold against his impressive upper torso.

"I'll have your tray delivered."

"Wait!" she called. Damn! Why had that come out sounding so desperate? "Why am I suddenly being allowed out?"

"To amuse me."

"Scre—"

"You *will* cease your habit of screaming vulgarities."

"Or?"

"Or I will give in to my urges and find something more useful for you to do with your mouth."

Kendall gaped at him. "Don't even think about it," she managed when she recovered from the shock of his suggestive remark.

Jonas crossed the room in three long strides. His hand went around her waist and he pulled her fully against him. He had every advantage. He outweighed her by at least a hundred pounds. He was at least a foot taller in height, and he had moved with such swiftness that Kendall hadn't even had a chance to turn away.

Her arms were pinned to her sides as he lifted her until they were at eye level. He smelled faintly of brandy. His eyes were steely gray, as hard and unyielding as his impressive body. His mouth was a thin, straight line. His eyes fell to her lips.

Nervously, Kendall's tongue flicked out to moisten her lower lip. Jonas stifled his groan. In spite of the rigidness of her small body, he saw that unmistakable passion in her smoldering blue eyes. He'd seen it that first night in the clearing. Had thought of little else these past weeks. This woman haunted him. He thought of her when he was awake, dreamed of her at night. It wasn't normal, and he knew he needed to get her out of his system so he could concentrate on his burdensome task. Maybe Rose was right; maybe she was some sort of witch.

He ravaged her mouth with his own. Jonas was so caught up in the taste of her that it took several protracted seconds for him to notice that she wasn't reacting. She was stiff in his arms. He thought of Cecelia and instantly set Kendall at arm's length.

He'd fully expected to see a bland expression, so the spark in her blue eyes surprised him. Schooling his grin, he lifted his palm to her cheek. Satisfaction welled within him when he noted the small shiver she was unable to conceal. Allowing the pad of his thumb to perform the most gentle caress, he held her gaze. Her skin was like silk, and warmed beneath his touch. He slowly continued the subtle exploration of her delicate cheek. Her breathing became more shallow, yet her expression never betrayed her thoughts. But her eyes did. Her wide eyes began to darken, turning to a rich azure that reflected the flames from the fireplace.

"You're beautiful," he whispered without realizing he had spoken aloud.

"You're arrogant."

He smiled at her proud response. "I think you like that."

"I think you need some sensitivity training."

He brought his other hand out and gently cupped her face, taking a step forward at the same time. "I think you'll find my... *training* satisfactory."

Dipping his head, he brushed her lips with his, careful to keep his body from touching hers. It took some effort, since he remembered all too well how she felt pressed against him. He nibbled her bottom lip, drawing it in with his teeth and teasing her with his tongue. His fingers wound into her mane of long blond hair, while his mouth continued to toy with hers. Jonas teased her and tasted her, waiting until the last possible second before actually moving to a kiss.

When he did, he was rewarded for his efforts. Kendall made a sound that teetered between a groan and a whimper, and her small hands flattened against his chest. Calling on all of his restraint, he gave her time to decide, sensing she was still considering pushing him away.

She surprised him when she lifted her arms around his neck and stepped into his embrace. It was his turn to swallow a groan at the pure pleasure of feeling her breasts pressed against chest. She was so small, yet there was a strength belying the frailty. He smiled mentally, knowing Kendall would take issue with being described as fragile.

His mind went blank when she pressed her hips to his, sending a surge of desire through him powerful enough to dismiss all rational thought. Jonas was only vaguely aware of lifting her and carrying her the few paces to the bed. Cautious of her size, he turned slightly so that he ended up on his back, with Kendall splayed on top of him. His hands explored her back, and suddenly he was annoyed that he had insisted she be dressed properly. He had never managed to forget the way he could feel every inch of her in her strange green outfit. Now his exploration was hindered by yards of fabric, corsets and—

"Revell!"

She broke out of his arms before his passion-drugged mind had fully come back to the present. As soon as he spotted the man and the woman in the bedroom, anger inspired reason.

"Grisom," he acknowledged as he threw one leg toward the edge of the bed and moved to a sitting position. "Rose," he added with a polite nod.

"I suggested he wait downstairs with the others, but he insisted on searching you out immediately." Rose offered a smug, knowing smile that did little to improve Jonas's mood.

His father-in-law was red faced, his cheeks puffed out with indignation. "What is the meaning of this?" he demanded.

"I should think that was obvious," Jonas answered as his eyes found Kendall. Seeing the apprehension on her face did little to improve his mood. He also couldn't help but notice—not without a fair amount of male pride—that she looked thoroughly kissed. Her thickly lashed eyes still held a flicker of passion and her hair was in wild disarray. Her chest rose and fell sharply with each breath and her hands were balled into tiny fists by her sides.

"I demand an explanation!" Harris Grisom yelled. For a small man, his voice certainly thundered.

"Now, Harris," Rose began as she looped her arm through his. "Calm down and we'll get this straightened out."

"He was—"

"I know what he was doing," Rose broke in with a quick look at Jonas. "But the bedroom is hardly an appropriate place for a discussion." Rose tugged the reluctant man, then glanced back over her shoulder to say, "Come along, Jonas, and bring her with you. This should be interesting."

As soon as they were alone, he turned to Kendall. "I suggest you do something with your hair and straighten your gown."

Her eyes spit fire at him. "Who was he?"

Jonas sighed. "My father-in-law."

"Then go on down," she told him, crossing her arms over her chest. "I'm sure he wants to talk to you, not me."

"And deprive you of suffering the wrath of the man along with me? No."

"Why would he care what you do?" Kendall argued as he led her out of the room.

"I suppose he feels affronted by my lack of mourning."

Kendall stopped abruptly. "Is that what this is all about?"

Jonas glared down at her. "If that is your way of asking if I was kissing you and thinking of Cecelia, I can assure you that was not the case."

"Jonas!" Rose called from below. "Hurry up!"

After Kendall fixed her hair and gown, she followed Jonas. As they reached the foyer, he heard Kendall gasp. One look in the parlor and he instantly knew the reason. Maitland was there, as were the Tanners and Captain William Whitefield. "If you breathe one word of what you saw out at Fairhaven," he said against her ear, "I'll kill you."

Chapter Four

"Shelby and Dylan," Kendall said on a breath.

"How do you know them?" Jonas demanded, tightening the grip on her elbow in the process.

Ignoring him, she rushed ahead, but stopped abruptly when Shelby Tanner stepped forward and said, "I'm sorry we haven't had an opportunity to be properly introduced."

"Shelby," Kendall cried. "Not you, too. God, I must be in Oz."

The brunette's smile barely faltered. "I'm afraid—"

"Explain yourself, Revell!" Harris Grisom bellowed from his position near the fireplace.

Kendall looked at the group, feeling all her old frustrations reignited. Shelby stood near Dylan, wearing the costume of the day. Maitland was dressed in a Confederate uniform, as was the man standing with him. Rose was smiling, but no one else was. They were too busy staring at her.

"Drink?" Jonas asked in a calm voice as he stepped to the bar and filled a leaded tumbler with some liquor from a decanter.

"This isn't a social call," the Confederate officer said.

"I thought as much," Jonas acknowledged with a sigh.

"You aren't going to like this," Rose warned as she lit the tip of her cigarette. "Whitefield has some rather interesting ideas."

"Do something, Dylan," Shelby urged.

"I'm Sheriff Tanner," Dylan said as he stepped forward. "And you are?"

"A friend of yours for years," she replied under her breath. Then, tightly, she met his eyes and said, "Kendall Butler." It was so hard to look at such a familiar face and feel as if she were looking into the eyes of a stranger. But that's what he was. What they all were. She had to get the locket back from Jonas. Then she could slip it over her head and end this strange nightmare.

"What brings you to Charleston?" Dylan asked.

"Who cares," Grisom interrupted. "Just arrest her."

"Arrest me?" Kendall said hotly. "What the hell for? I'm the one who has been locked—"

"What is all this, Harris?" Rose interrupted. "You can't have the girl arrested for kissing Jonas. If you arrested every woman who's kissed him, Dylan would have to build a new jail."

The little man turned a brighter shade of red. "Tell them, Whitefield."

"Ma'am, I'm Captain Whitefield, Third Regiment."

Kendall stared up at the well-dressed, attractive man she guessed was somewhere around her age. He had thick, blond hair and expressive blue eyes. Had he not been staring down at her with such hatred, she might have found him attractive.

"Congratulations," she murmured, feeling the need to lash out at him.

"You're under arrest."

He started to reach for her, when Jonas suddenly stepped forward, placing his large body between them. "What is this all about, Whitefield?"

Kendall could feel the unbridled tension as the two men's eyes locked. If Whitefield had viewed her with hatred, there wasn't an adjective that could describe the look he gave Jonas. The man's eyes filled with rage as they narrowed.

"Stay out of this, Revell. Or I'll arrest you, too."

"Dylan!" Shelby wailed.

"You're welcome to try," Jonas said as a dangerous light turned his eyes the color of the sky before a violent storm.

"Captain Whitefield, what is this all about?" Rose asked as she moved closer and blew a stream of smoke at the two men. "For what reason could you possibly wish to arrest Kendall?"

"Treason."

"What?" Kendall scoffed. "That's the craziest pile of cra—"

"Kendall!" Jonas admonished.

"She's right," Rose offered with an incredibly inappropriate lightness in her tone. "Where did you get this ridiculous notion from?"

"She was identified."

"By whom?" Kendall cut in. "The only people I've met are—"

"What do you mean, 'identified'?" Jonas demanded.

Kendall noticed that Jonas sent a look, menacing and quick, in Maitland's direction.

"My regiment captured one of the Yankees responsible for firing on your plantation. Before he died, he admitted the cannon fire was supposed to cover up a meeting between a Northern sympathizer and one of their people. He couldn't give us any names, but he said he saw the woman."

Whitefield turned his angry, blue eyes on Kendall before he continued. "He said the woman was small and had blond hair."

"You're arresting me because of my hair color?" Kendall asked. "If that isn't bull—"

"Kendall!" Rose said sharply. "Captain, that does seem rather... incredible."

"The man described you perfectly," Whitefield insisted, undeterred. His eyes roamed over Kendall in a very derogatory manner. "He said you wore your hair in a fashion appropriate for the bedchamber."

Jonas didn't waste any time grabbing the man by the lapels of his uniform. "You'll regret that, Whitefield," he seethed between clenched teeth.

"Gentlemen," Shelby urged softly as Dylan went behind Jonas and placed one hand on his shoulder.

"I'm afraid your prisoner must have been mistaken," Rose announced on a breath. "Kendall couldn't possibly have anything to do with treason."

"She was seen," Grisom stubbornly insisted. "You heard the man yourself, Maitland. You knew he was describing this . . . woman immediately. You even told Captain Whitefield she was here with Revell."

"You?" Kendall accused, narrowing her eyes to glare at Maitland. "I can't believe you would—"

She didn't get to finish the thought, because Jonas turned and gave her a warning look. *Great*, she groaned inwardly. *If I tell them it was Maitland and Jonas, Jonas will kill me. If I don't say anything, Whitefield will arrest me and Lord knows what else.*

"I can assure you that Kendall has no part in this," Rose began.

"I know your feelings for Jonas," Grisom warned.

"But you obviously don't know my relationship to Kendall."

The two women's eyes met and Kendall could see that Rose was lying. There was no flicker of recognition.

"Kendall is a distant niece," she continued.

"That still doesn't mean she wasn't consorting with the enemy," Whitefield sneered.

"The only one she's been consorting with is Jonas," Rose argued, ignoring the shocked faces of the men in the room.

"You admit it, then," Grisom spat. "You brought a wh—"

"Don't finish that," Jonas warned.

"Harris," Rose said, sighing. "Because we've known each other since childhood, I'll overlook your lack of manners toward a member of my family."

"That appears to be a sound idea," Shelby offered. "Perhaps we should all take a deep breath and approach this more reasonably."

"Being your niece might explain why she is here, but it certainly doesn't explain why she was seen at Fairhaven," Grisom challenged.

Rose moved over and placed her arm around Kendall's shoulder. "Kendall's family has suffered some financial setbacks," Rose lied. "They placed this girl in a very delicate position, and I considered it my duty to do what I could."

"What position?" Kendall whispered, ignoring the elbow Rose delivered as warning.

"Her father, being unable to see to her basic comforts, felt it was long past appropriate for Kendall to marry."

"Marry?" Kendall repeated hoarsely.

"Yes, dear," Rose said with stern caution in her eyes. "I know you've always likened matrimony to death, but I can assure you, the alternative would be quite unpleasant."

Kendall gave her that point. Especially when she looked up to see Whitefield and Grisom just waiting to cart her out of there.

"After discussing the matter with Jonas," Rose continued, casting the large man a look similar to the one she'd given Kendall, "we decided that instead of Kendall being forced to advertise for a husband, she would suit Jonas."

"But— Ouch!" Kendall exclaimed when Rose allowed the heel of her boot to come down on Kendall's toes.

"You expect us to believe that she was incapable of finding a husband without resorting to trickery?" Whitefield asked.

"Hardly. But as you might have guessed by her rather colorful vocabulary, Kendall has never wished to tie herself to a man."

"And she has no intention of marrying a man who tied her up," she said under her breath.

"You see?" Shelby asked brightly. "I knew there was a logical explanation for everything."

"I won't have it!" Grisom exploded. "It isn't proper! Cecelia isn't even cold in her grave."

"Calm down, Harris. This really shouldn't concern you. Jonas shouldn't be expected to climb into the grave with her."

"Why not?" Grisom countered. "He put her there."

"Enough, Harris," Dylan said. "I think we've settled this matter. I'll see you out."

"And I'll see him dead for what he did to my Cecelia."

"Shelby is married to Dylan, and you still want me to believe that this is 1861?" Kendall demanded as soon as she and Rose were alone.

She felt the woman give her a withering look.

"You aren't going to start all that again, are you? It really is growing tiresome."

"Then give me some reasonable explanation for all this," Kendall pleaded. "I know everybody—no one knows me. Everybody looks and acts the same, but they aren't the same."

"The same as what?" Rose asked. "You keep going on about *your* time and *my* time and Jonas will have you committed. Besides, you should be more worried about Grisom and Whitehall than about whom Shelby has chosen to marry."

"Is Grisom the one who shot Jonas?" Kendall asked Rose a few minutes later.

Rose shrugged. "Probably. He's taken his daughter's death very hard."

"Did Jonas kill her?"

Rose leveled her green gaze on Kendall. "I suggest you ask him yourself."

"You're assuming he'll speak to me again. Or didn't you catch his expression before he stormed over to pout in the corner?"

Rose's smile was slightly tempered. "He's just angry because he's probably feeling that he's being manipulated into marriage for the second time in as many months."

"We aren't going to get married," Kendall announced. "I'll do anything to keep that from happening."

"You're welcome to try," Jonas said from the distant corner of the candlelit room.

Turning, she met his stony expression and matched it with one of her own. "Don't be a jacka— Ridiculous," she amended. "You don't want to marry me any more than I want to marry you."

"True."

"Then we'll just forget this, here and now."

"No, we won't." There was such finality in his tone that Kendall actually shuddered.

"I will not marry you and you can't force me to," she said, squaring her shoulders and lifting her chin.

"Goodbye, Rose," Jonas said, without letting his eyes leave Kendall's face.

"Stay, Rose."

Jonas's eyes narrowed ever so slightly. "Now."

"Good luck," Rose muttered as she hurriedly made her escape.

"Look, Jonas," Kendall began when they were alone. "I don't know why you're being so damned diff—"

"Are you capable of uttering a single sentence without a curse in it?"

Smiling, she said, "Hell, no."

"You are exasperating, woman," he grumbled as he crossed the room and refilled his glass. "We will be married just as soon as I can make the arrangements."

"Listen to me," Kendall said as she tilted her head up to meet Jonas's eyes. "I know this sounds nuts, but somehow I've shown up here. I don't know how or why. I'm not even sure any of this is real. But I do know that the last thing I did before this happened was put on that locket. If you'll just hand me back the locket, hopefully I can undo whatever I did." she gave him a pleading smile. "No Kendall, no forced wedding. And we're both happy."

Jonas looked at her then, and she suddenly saw fatigue on his handsome features. It was so pronounced that she actually thought about going over to him and giving him a reassuring hug. But she knew better.

"I think it would be best for all of us if we simply played out the scenario Rose created."

"We can't get married," Kendall insisted. "I don't know what happened—it goes against everything I was ever taught or believed—but I know I don't belong here."

"I agree."

"You believe me?" she asked, shocked. "I can't tell you—"

"Do I believe that you're some sort of aberration from the future?" he asked with a great deal of sarcasm. "I might have, until I felt you, kissed you. You're definitely real."

Warm color heated her cheeks and it made Kendall wonder when the last time was she'd actually blushed. "Give me the locket and I can prove it," she challenged.

Downing the contents of the glass in one swallow, Jonas dug into the pocket of his vest and pulled out the locket, allowing it to dangle tauntingly from one square-tipped finger. His dark hair, caught in a string of soft rawhide at his nape, swayed with the movement of his neck.

Grudgingly, Kendall moved forward, but she wasn't about to give the man the satisfaction of begging. Instead, she simply offered her palm and met his gray gaze. She was close enough to feel the heat emanating from his large body. Close enough to smell his brandy-scented breath. Close enough for her pulse to quicken from the memory of his searing kiss.

After a brief, silent clash, Jonas allowed the locket to fall into her opened palm. Kendall wasted no time. Closing her eyes, she slipped the chain over her head and waited. Nothing.

Holding her breath, she placed her fingers on the pendant and squeezed it tightly.

"You're still here," Jonas said with faint amusement.

"It has to work," she insisted. "I got here by putting this thing on. It has to be the key to ending this nightmare. I have to get back to where I belong."

"It seems your mode of . . . transportation has failed you."

"Stop laughing at me," she warned. "I would think you'd be thrilled to have me disappear. Then you wouldn't have to marry me."

"It wouldn't be my choice, but then I'm not sure I could carry out the alternative."

"Which is?"

A long pause forced her pulse to a more erratic beat. "I can either marry you or kill you," he explained calmly.

Kendall's frustration grew into anger. Locking her eyes with his, she lifted her chin and asked, "Is that the same bargain you had with your first wife?"

He shrugged. "Since she's dead, I would think the answer rather obvious."

Chapter Five

"What is it?" Jonas asked. The harsh tone he'd used on Kendall lessened when he looked toward the doorway and noticed the slumped shoulders of the very distraught Mrs. McCafferty.

"I've word from the midwife," she said, her green eyes wide with fear and flowing tears. "My Colleen's time is here."

She watched Jonas's dark features soften before he moved quickly to the woman's side. "Calm yourself. There is no—"

"There's trouble," Mrs. McCafferty blurted out as she fell against Jonas's chest. Deep sobs rocked her body. "The doctor has seen to her. He said there was no hope left."

"What's the problem, Mrs. McCafferty?" Kendall asked as she took a step closer to the woman in order to place a hand on her heaving shoulder.

"My child is dying. My poor baby is dying."

Kendall's fingers gripped a bit more urgently. "What is it?"

"The birthing," Mrs. McCafferty said through her sobs. "I thought all along she was just too frail for such hardship."

"I can help her."

Kendall expected them to dismiss her with nothing more than a curt grunt, since it was their usual response. Jonas appeared as if he might do just that.

"Yes," Mrs. McCafferty said, hope springing to the eyes she was wiping on the sleeve of her plain gown. "I watched how you tended His Lordship. Maybe you can work a miracle on my Colleen, as well."

"No miracles," Kendall cautioned. "But the faster we get there, the better." Kendall remained still for a minute, then reeled off a list of things she would need. Jonas still didn't move. "I can't keep her from dying if you stand rooted in that spot."

"Please?" Mrs. McCafferty added as she looked up at her employer. "I'll gladly extend my service if you'll allow your fiancée to aid my daughter."

Fiancée. Kendall shivered at the sound of the word. Whether it was the urging from his housekeeper or the challenge she offered with her eyes, Jonas reached for their cloaks and started toward the back of the house.

"We'd better stay off the main road," he said. "I'm not fully convinced that Whitefield and Grisom wouldn't try something."

"Like what?" Kendall asked, struggling against the yards of fabric in order to keep pace with the big man.

"We can discuss it later."

Kendall rolled her eyes as she ran to keep from falling behind. Nothing seemed even vaguely familiar. The streets were little more than even stone and dirt, and the stench was almost overwhelming.

Kendall was relieved to find that they didn't have far to go. Following Jonas and Mrs. McCafferty, she stepped into a chilly home that seemed crowded and somber. By the light of the fire, Kendall could see the young girl, probably no more than fifteen. Her sweat-matted hair was strawberry blond and her face was as white as the ashes lining the hearth. A substantial amount of blood had already been lost.

Dropping her cloak on the way, Kendall went to the girl, ripped the sheet aside and felt for a pulse. "It's weak, but still there. We'll have to work fast to save them."

"Them?" came a shocked woman's voice.

Kendall turned toward the sound and found a pair of hostile brown eyes glaring at her. "Are you the midwife?"

The woman straightened indignantly. "I am. And I've vast experience with this sort of—"

"Go to Rose and get some ether, a sieve and some muslin."

"I'll not be taking orders from the likes of you!" she exclaimed.

"Miss Whitefield," Jonas began in a controlled voice. "Miss Butler is quite well trained in such matters. Since you've obviously done all that is in your power, I think it only appropriate that we see what else can be done."

"But to try to save the mother and not the baby is a sin against God."

"I plan on saving them both," Kendall snapped. "So either do as I ask, or get the hell out of my way." She moved to the end of the sheet, lifting it in order to do a pelvic. "Damn it," she muttered. "The baby is breech and this woman isn't even the least bit dilated or effaced."

She looked up, to find Jonas and Mrs. McCafferty gaping at her. "The baby is turned around the wrong way and the birth canal isn't open," she translated.

Mrs. McCafferty fell into a fit of gut-wrenching sobs. Miss Whitefield almost looked smug. Apparently, she had guessed as much.

The woman on the table moaned softly.

"She's hemorrhaging, so we have to get going." No one moved. Kendall looked from person to person, saving Jonas for last. "I would think the fact that your punctured lung has healed would be proof enough of my skill and training. If this woman and her child die, I hope it haunts you forever."

His gray eyes locked with hers. "Go!" he growled at the midwife. "Jeffreys is outside. Have him assist you, but be quick about it."

Kendall checked the girl's pulse again, disappointed when it felt weaker. "Hang in there," she said gently. "You and your baby will be just fine if you stay with me just a little longer."

"Is that true?"

A small shiver danced along her spine when she heard Jonas's softly spoken question. "If we get started in time. And if I can get to all the bleeders before it's too late."

"Bleeders?"

Kendall moved to place both hands on the girl's distended abdomen. "The blood vessels that nourish the baby in the womb. If I can't repair them in time, she'll bleed to death."

Mrs. McCafferty sobbed. "Please, miss. Colleen is all I have in this world."

The return of Miss Whitefield and the supplies saved Kendall from having to lie to the woman. Colleen was hemorrhaging so badly that she knew it would be a miracle if she lived.

"What are you doing?" Miss Whitefield shrieked when Kendall tore the cotton gown covering Colleen. "How can you humiliate the girl? You can't mean to leave her exposed when the priest—"

"Shut up!" Kendall commanded between tightly clenched teeth. "Jonas, take the muslin, fasten it over the sieve and hold it firmly over Colleen's mouth. Cover your own mouth and nose, as well."

"Why?"

"To keep her from regaining consciousness when I take the baby, and to keep you from falling over on top of her from breathing in the anesthetic."

"Oh, God," Miss Whitefield managed before she fainted into a heap on the dusty floor.

"Isn't there another way?" Jonas asked, a twinge of reluctance in his deep voice.

"You could punch her," Kendall suggested. "But I didn't think you'd feel right about knocking her out like that."

She hid her satisfaction as she watched Jonas position the sieve above the girl's pale face.

"You only give one additional drop of ether if you see signs of her regaining consciousness," Kendall warned. "We don't want to drug the baby if we can help it."

Kendall stood and went to the pot by the fire and did her best to sterilize the implements, as well as her own hands. "What I wouldn't give for one decent clamp," she grumbled. "Mrs. McCafferty, you'll have to help me."

"Anything."

"Keep those bandages handy. When I tell you to apply pressure, you do it immediately, okay?"

The older woman nodded.

"Then—" Kendall took in a deep breath "—we're ready."

Kendall stood over the girl, blade in her hand. Just before making the incision, she looked over at Jonas. Concern had formed deep lines on either side of his eyes. His mouth was little more than a taut line beneath the swatch of transparent muslin. Still, he offered a slight incline with his dark head and Kendall began.

Colleen moaned as the incision was made. "Ether, Jonas. Just one drop."

"Done."

"Watch her eyelids," Kendall called as she held out her hand for one of the cloth bandages. "Hold it here," she told Mrs. McCafferty. "Press gently but firmly."

"I don't know if I can," she admitted.

"Jeffreys!" Jonas bellowed. The man came in immediately. "Take Mrs. McCafferty's place."

"Yes, sir."

Kendall was vaguely aware of the shuffle of feet as her new assistant took his place beside her. "Like old times?" she asked.

"Yes, Madame," he said. His hand went to the bandage and he applied pressure just as he had on the night they had worked on Jonas.

"Are you still with us, Mrs. McCafferty?" Kendall called a few minutes later.

"Yes" came the weak reply.

"Get ready," Kendall instructed. A few seconds later, she lifted a perfectly formed baby boy from his mother's womb. After cutting the cord and tying it off, she tipped the baby to rid him of fluids, then gave his backside a resounding whack. Nothing.

Cursing, she placed the still-wet infant on his mother's belly and began CPR. Fifteen, sixteen, short breaths...and then it happened. He let out a fierce cry that made Kendall want to cry, as well.

"Wrap him up and get him near the fire," she instructed.

"But Colleen?" Mrs. McCafferty asked, her joy tempered by her anxiousness for her deathly still daughter.

"She's next on my list," Kendall assured the woman, with more confidence than she actually felt.

"You can do it," Jonas said from his position near Colleen's head.

"Let's hope," she answered, grateful for that small boost in her confidence. How could such an arrogant man know just the right thing to say?

The damage to Colleen's body was extensive. It took Kendall almost two hours to locate and repair all the torn blood vessels, along with the tear in the girl's uterus. The blood vessels would heal; the damage to her uterus might mean that Colleen would never have another baby.

"She'll wake up in a few minutes," Kendall finally told Mrs. McCafferty. Seeing the woman's hesitation, she added, "It's only the ether."

"Bless you," Mrs. McCafferty gushed, dropping to her knees to hug Kendall's legs. "I owe you my life."

Kendall pulled the woman to her feet. "You don't owe me anything, but there are some things you need to do for Colleen."

"Anything," Mrs. McCafferty promised. "I can't believe you saved my daughter and the babe. Surely it's a miracle."

"It's a C-section," Kendall said with a sigh. "Make sure Miss Whitefield keeps the baby warm, and if he gets hungry, take him to Colleen, even if she's asleep."

Kendall glanced over at the midwife, who was cradling the quiet baby. At least the woman was good for something.

"I'll be back to check on her. Just follow the instructions I laid out for you earlier, and Colleen and the baby will be fine," Kendall assured the grateful woman clutching her hand.

"Then you must be as you say you are," she said. "You've got the gift of healing."

"Nothing so ethereal, I'm afraid. I was educated at—"

"We'll be going now," Jonas said as his hand suddenly appeared at Kendall's elbow. "Stay here with your daughter."

With a cape draped across her shoulders to ward off the evening chill, Kendall followed Jonas from the house. The streets were deserted in the early-morning hours, which somehow made Kendall feel her fatigue more acutely.

"Would you mind slowing to a sprint?" she asked irritably. Jonas was already several paces ahead of her.

"Sprint?" he repeated, his features shrouded by the brim of his hat.

"I'm tired. I don't feel like jogging all the way back to the Rose Tattoo."

With a reluctant shrug of his broad shoulders, Jonas waited for her to come up beside him before continuing at a more reasonable pace.

Kendall tried not to think about him. She wasn't very successful, though. She kept glancing at his profile out the corner of her eye. His near-perfect posture made him move with grace and arrogance.

They had gone less than a block, when he spoke. "What is sprint, and why do you insist on calling my home by that awful name?"

"Sprint is a long-distance carrier," she answered, just to be obstinate.

"What?"

"Forget it. I was just trying to explain to you that I didn't feel like running just to keep up with you."

"My apologies."

"You need to work on your delivery, Jonas," she chided. "You don't sound very apologetic."

"Perhaps it has something to do with our current circumstances."

She heard the derision in his voice and it rankled. "I'm not real thrilled with things, either," she assured him. "If you think you're being inconvenienced, try being transported in time to a place without a hair dryer or dental floss."

She felt the pinch of his hands grasping her arms as he yanked her off the walkway and shoved her against a building. She didn't need to see his eyes to feel them boring into her. The short, irritated breaths told her he was angry.

"Let go!" she demanded.

"Be quiet," he countered with a gentle shake. "I haven't yet discovered your game, but I will not allow you to continue this nonsense about time travel and such."

"You will not allow?" Kendall repeated. "I don't really give a damn what you will or won't allow. All I care about is figuring out how to get back to where I belong and away from *you*."

Several tense seconds passed when neither spoke. It was a classic standoff, and an even more classic battle of wills. And Kendall was determined not to blink first.

"It's late," Jonas said as his hands fell away from her arms. "Hurry."

With that, he turned and briskly walked through the darkness, leaving Kendall to follow. She lingered against the building, weighing her options and battling with the anger still churning in her stomach. Maybe she should go to Rose's shop.

The thought brightened her spirits remarkably. "Which way, though?" she whispered as she tried to find her bearings in the darkness. It wasn't an easy task. The Charleston she inhabited was nothing like this. All she knew was that Rose's apothecary was across the street from the Tattoo.

Lifting the hems of the many annoying layers of skirts, Kendall followed the direction where Jonas had disappeared, wishing she had taken the time to memorize their route on the way to attend Colleen's labor.

She was aided in her trek by dim candlelight from some of the homes, but she felt strangely ill at ease. *This isn't my time,* she reminded herself. *I don't think muggers have been invented yet—at least, I hope not.*

Her footsteps echoed against the stone street. It seemed like a cruel reminder that she was alone. She quickened her pace, keeping close to the buildings and their ornate fences. She paused briefly at each street corner, trying to find her way. She stopped once, just to see if she could hear the sound of Jonas's footsteps ahead. Nothing.

Anxiety quickly gave way to annoyance when she knew she was lost in the back alleys of the city. "Just one more reason to hate that man," she grumbled as she decided to turn left at the next corner. She was fairly certain that she needed to go east. She was less certain that east was to the left, but she figured she had a fifty-fifty shot.

The turn placed her on a wider residential street, lined by large homes with arches and gated gardens. Breathing a sigh of relief, Kendall was assured she was headed in the right general direction. All she needed to do was find the lights from the harbor and she could work her way back.

She reached the third cross street, when she felt a hand touch her shoulder from behind.

She fairly jumped at the unexpected contact. "I swear, Revell—"

"Don't turn around, Miss Butler."

Kendall didn't recognize the voice beyond the fact that the speaker was a woman.

"If you marry Jonas, I'll kill you."

and southern accent."

Chapter Six

"Who the hell are you?" Kendall demanded as she
shrugged off the hand and turned to face the woman.

A very feminine gasp fell from beneath the black veil
covering the face. The woman was much taller than
Kendall, but apparently not terribly assertive. She
cowered against the stone arch almost instantly.

"I asked you a question," Kendall repeated more
forcefully. She took a step closer, which seemed to send
the woman into a panic.

"I . . . meant . . . what . . . I . . . said," she stammered
in a cultured Southern accent.

"Jeez," Kendall groaned as she reached forward and
ripped the veil and hat from the woman's head. Ignoring her second gasp, Kendall tossed the items into the
gutter. "Now, can we stop playing cloak and dagger
and will you tell me why you're threatening me?"

Light from a window above the garden cast a yel-
lowish shadow across the woman's face. Not woman,
Kendall amended mentally—girl. She looked to be
somewhere around seventeen or eighteen, tops. She

also looked scared to death, if the paleness of her skin was any indication.

"You can't harm me, Miss Butler."

Kendall rolled her eyes. "You're the one making death threats."

"I can't let you marry Jonas."

"Then we have some common ground," Kendall muttered.

The girl's expression brightened. "But Father said you—"

"Father?" Kendall interrupted.

"Harris Grisom is my father."

"And you are?"

"Caroline Grisom."

"Okay, so now I understand why you don't want me to marry Jonas, but I—"

"Jonas loves me," the girl blurted out.

"Time out," Kendall said. Instantly seeing the confusion register on the girl's face, she translated her slang. "Wait a minute. Wasn't Jonas married to your sister?"

The girl's lashes fluttered as her eyes dropped. "That was Father's doing."

"But your father said Jonas killed your sister."

The girl's face instantly closed as she hurriedly turned away. "I have to go," Caroline said as she slipped inside the gate and secured the latch.

Kendall considered calling her back or even pounding on the gate, but she didn't dare if there was a chance Harris Grisom was in the vicinity. That man wanted her arrested by the Confederacy.

"There you are!" Jonas growled. "What are you doing all the way over here?"

"Being threatened by your sweet, young plaything," she replied caustically.

"This is not the best place for us to be," he warned as he came up beside her.

"Do the Grisoms live here?" she inquired, pointing toward the house.

She could see his eyebrows pull together in confusion. "Not Grisom. Franklin Monroe."

"Who is he?" she asked as Jonas cupped her elbow and hurried her into the shadows and down the street.

"He's a barrister. He works closely with the Confederate regiment here in Charleston, acting as a prosecutor in civil matters."

"What's your girlfriend doing hanging at his place?"

"Who was hanged?" he asked, stopping in his tracks.

"Not hanging as in execution. Hanging as in hanging around. Staying with him."

"What girlfriend?"

"Your sister-in-law," Kendall answered in a singsong voice intended to irritate him. "Caroline, the one who looked young enough to be your daughter."

Jonas said nothing as they zigzagged through the streets until they reached the back entrance of the Rose Tattoo. After seeing her inside, he lit several lamps, which filled the first floor with light.

Kendall tossed her cape over the back of a chair and started for the stairs.

"Where do you think you're going?"

"To bed," she answered flatly, not turning to face him. Placing her foot on the tread of the first step, she added, "I've had a rather trying night."

"Then you must appreciate how my life has been these past few weeks."

I don't care! she silently screamed. *I don't even hear a twinge of sadness and loneliness in his voice. The man is an aberration and I'm having a hallucination. Maybe when I wake up in the morning, all this will be over.*

"Please stay."

He asked in a voice so soft she almost didn't hear him.

Against her better judgment, she joined him in the drawing room. Kendall found him stirring the fire back to life. In no time flames crackled as the fire danced along the edges of the logs, adding a genuine warmth to the room. Kendall moved to stand near the hearth, only now realizing that she was chilled. Her eyes follow Jonas as he went and poured two glasses of brandy.

"I shouldn't," she said as he held out the glass to her.

One dark brow arched as he asked, "You don't care for spirits?"

"It's the glass," she admitted with a small smile. "And the decanter. The lead from leaded crystal actually seeps into whatever is stored there. Lead poisoning has been proved to cause everything from brain damage to learning disabilities."

Jonas smiled as he shook his head; amusement lightened his sad, gray eyes. "You truly do have an odd base of knowledge, Miss Butler. If I didn't know better, I might actually believe your claims of being from another time."

"What would it take to convince you?" Kendall countered, accepting the glass and sipping the brandy while she awaited his answer.

"This is a frivolous conversation," he hedged.

"You're the one who wanted to talk, so talk. Tell me what I would have to do to convince you that I am from the 1990s?"

"Will this war be over quickly, as so many of my fellow Southerners believe?"

Kendall placed her glass on the mantel and tried not to think about how devastatingly handsome he looked in his dark jacket, white shirt and black ascot. She had to try harder when he shrugged out of the jacket, leaving her an unobstructed view of his well-developed upper body encased in fine silk.

"Of course not," she said softly, meeting his eyes. "This war lasts until 1865. But you don't have to worry. For some reason known only to God and General Sherman, he spares Charleston and burns Columbia, instead. Of course, he does a real number on Atlanta."

She watched as his expression darkened. Immediately, she felt herself grow defensive. "So don't believe me—I don't really give a damn."

"Who taught you to speak in such, er, colorful terms?"

"College, I guess. Most of my buddies were guys, so I seem to have picked up some of their bad habits."

"It really isn't befitting a proper Southern lady."

"I'm not a proper Southern lady, Jonas. I'm a forensic pathologist."

"A what?"

"A doctor who performs medical-legal autopsies. I've only been—"

"You mean to tell me that you perform surgery on the dead?"

"I examine the remains of the deceased to determine cause and manner of death."

"Who would allow such a thing?"

Kendall laughed. "Don't look so disgusted, Jonas. In my time, what I do is considered a great service to the community. You remember I mentioned Mr. Hines?"

"The man who supposedly gave you Cecelia's locket?"

Kendall bristled, but she let the barb pass. "His infant son was found dead in his crib. The police were ready to charge him and his wife with the murder of the baby boy. Autopsy showed that the baby died from SIDS."

"SIDS?"

"It's a terrible condition that seems to strike babies in their first year. They simply stop breathing and die."

"And you can tell such a thing just by examining the . . . corpse?"

Kendall didn't think he was ready to hear all about the actual steps in the autopsy procedure, so she just said, "I do a very thorough examination."

Jonas tugged the rawhide lace from his hair, then raked his fingers nervously through the long, ebony strands. "You're very convincing."

"Then you believe me, finally?"

His smile was just a tad patronizing. "You haven't told me anything that I can actually verify."

"Okay," Kendall began. "This is the end of November. On December 11, half this city will burn to the ground."

"Really, Kendall," he snorted, obviously unconvinced.

"Yes, *really,*" she snapped. "The fire will start at night near the foot of Hasell Street."

"Why? What starts the fire?"

"No one really knew," she answered. "The theory was that the Confederate troops were angry when they couldn't get you wealthy folks to hand over your slaves to help them in The Cause." She sneered through the last of her comment, hoping he might comprehend that she actually did know what she was talking about.

Jonas fell into a chair, his large frame filling the small piece of furniture. He downed the rest of his drink in a single swallow.

"Oh, and you really should send your valuables north for the duration of the war. Pillaging will be rampant when things start to heat up."

"If what you're saying is true, it will be like Scotland all over again."

"Excuse me?"

"The British Isles have been sacking one another for centuries. I was raised on tales of the horrors of civil war."

"You're British?"

"Half."

"You don't look very European," Kendall remarked.

The grin he offered was almost boyish in its charm. "My father found his bride here in America."

"You don't look very American, either."

"I should," he countered. "My mother was half American, half Navajo. I think that allows me a certain right to claim this land as my own."

"Point. But since the South is going to be a nasty place for the next four years, why don't you just go back to England until the worst is over."

"And do what?"

"I heard Mrs. McCafferty call you a lord. Can't you go back and lord over something?"

"I am my father's fifth son. My usefulness in England pales badly in comparison with what I am doing here."

"Which is?"

He regarded her for a long, silent moment. "Currently, I'm planning on marrying you."

"I was being serious."

"As was I," he assured her with an annoying inclination of his dark head.

"I will do anything to keep from marrying you."

"You're welcome to try."

"I won't have to try very hard," she told him. "I'll simply refuse."

"It won't matter. Dylan Tanner is the closest thing we have to law right now. Your refusal won't matter much to him."

"Dylan isn't like that," she insisted, setting her glass down on the end table beside her. That got his attention. "Dylan is a kind, fair man who won't idly sit by and let any man force any woman into *anything*. Especially not a marriage."

Jonas sighed. "But he will."

"Will not."

"He will when he understands that the alternative is that I turn you over to Captain Whitefield to be tried for treason."

"Jonas!" she cried, rushing over to kneel in front of him. Without thinking, Kendall placed her hands atop his, but removed them immediately when she felt the warm abrasiveness of his skin. "It seems to me that you already have a boatload of troubles in this town. The last thing you need is some sham marriage that will only irritate Grisom and his Confederate cronies."

Jonas leaned forward and lifted her, pulling her into his lap. His brandy-scented breath filled the air separating their faces. Kendall felt the muscles of his thighs beneath her bottom and the hardness of his chest where she was pressed against him. Her body reacted, warming her all over and inspiring her heart rate to a new level.

Catching a lock of her hair between his thumb and forefinger, Jonas studied it for a moment before turning those bone-melting gray eyes on her. "Sham, Kendall?"

Flattening her palms against his chest, she gave a small push. It proved to be a futile effort. Jonas had wrapped his hand around her waist, and was holding her firmly in place. "Don't do this," she warned, wondering why so little of her mental conviction had found its way into her tone.

"Don't do this?" he repeated as his lips brushed against her cheek. "Or this?" he whispered just before delivering the most feather-light kiss she had ever experienced.

His fingers moved through her hair, gently pushing aside the long mass to position her mouth beneath his. The sensations came in a burst of light and fire. Warmth traveled from her slightly parted lips through to the very core of her being. A moan rumbled in her throat when his tongue flicked out to tease her.

As if acting of their own volition, Kendall's hands slid up over the sculpted hardness of his chest to the corded muscle at his shoulders. Clutching his shirt, she held on as his mouth took her to a new place. Every cell in her body was filled with an unfamiliar longing. It was a fierce need that seemed fully capable of short-circuiting all her brain functions.

Slowly, Jonas lifted his head, revealing half-closed eyes that shimmered with unfulfilled passion. "I don't believe 'sham' is an apt description."

The even tone of his delivery belied the look in his eyes. It did, however, completely douse her desires. "How about farce, then?" she asked smartly. "Why don't you just marry Caroline? She's definitely interested.''

"She's a child," he said with a dismissive shake of his head.

"Isn't that how you people like them? Young and stupid?''

"You people?"

"Your culture," she corrected as she got to her feet. Part of her was annoyed that she hadn't done so sooner. Yet another part was disappointed when he made no move to stop her. "Aren't you supposed to be married by the age of twelve or something?''

"How old are you?" he asked conversationally.

His sudden change in mood was baffling and a bit irritating. "I'm twenty-seven."

"You can kiss like that and you've never been married?" he asked with so much astonishment that you'd have thought she'd just told him she had three legs.

"Nope. I've never wanted to be married."

His expression deteriorated. "You're not . . ."

"No wonder you and Rose get along so well. Yes, Jonas, I am heterosexual."

"Hetero . . ."

"My sexual preference is men."

Kendall derived great pleasure from watching the faint pink stain crawl across his bronzed cheeks. "How about you?" she continued. "Are you straight?"

"Straight?"

"Do your sexual tastes run toward women, or do you—"

"I believe I have already proved myself, Miss Butler."

It was Kendall's turn to blush. "Let's call this one a draw."

"Yes, let's. I've made arrangements for you to be fitted for a gown at Shelby's shop tomorrow—rather, this afternoon," he said as he noted the pastel sky signaling the break of day.

"Gown for what?"

"For the wedding."

"Shelby makes dresses?" Kendall asked, truly shocked. "I can't imagine her with a needle and thread in hand."

His frown was deep and conveyed his feelings perfectly. "She runs the shop. She's made quite a success of it."

"Too bad *The Wizard of Oz* doesn't come out for another seventy-eight years. Dorothy had the same trouble I seem to be having. Except I don't think I can click my heels together and get back to Kansas."

"So you're actually from Kansas?"

"*Dorothy* was from Kansas." She groaned in frustration. "I was just trying to make a point. A point I can't make without explaining too many other things. Dorothy is a fictional character who hits her head and has a dream that's filled with people she knows, but they don't know her. Just like Rose, Shelby and Dylan have no idea who I am, but I know all about them."

"You are a gifted storyteller, Miss Butler."

"Right, that's how I was able to save your life and Colleen's." Grabbing her skirts, Kendall prepared to stomp off.

"I never did thank you," he said to her back.

"No, you didn't."

"I do appreciate what you did, Kendall."

"I would have done the same thing for anyone," she responded flatly. "Even Captain Whitefield. It is what I'm trained to do."

"I'll keep that in mind. Perhaps you can offer your services to The Cause after the wedding."

"There isn't going to be a wedding," Kendall stated firmly.

"Yes, there is. The day after tomorrow at noon."

Chapter Seven

"Was it you?" Jonas asked as he regarded the stubby man in the chair across from him. The generous amount of perspiration beading on Maitland's balding head didn't escape Jonas's notice.

"Of course not," he answered forcefully. "I need you too much to do something as stupid as killing you. But the woman is another matter altogether."

It took a great deal of effort to keep his expression bland. "Miss Butler is not a topic for open discussion. I believe we were discussing—"

"You might have fooled Whitefield and Grisom, but I was there, Revell. Miss Butler was not wandering around Fairhaven that night in search of a husband."

Jonas smiled and let out a slow breath. "What can I say. She simply misunderstood Mrs. Porter's instructions and went to Fairhaven instead of meeting me here in town. A simple matter of miscommunication."

"You expect me to believe that you actually intend to marry that woman?"

"Tomorrow, as planned," Jonas replied. "Neither of us sees any valid reason to delay, what with the war and all."

Maitland rose and began to pace nervously. "This wasn't part of our arrangement, Revell. How can I be assured that your... bride won't destroy everything we've put into place?"

"I am fully capable of controlling my wife."

Maitland smiled appreciatively. "You did a fine job with the first one."

Jonas felt every muscle in his body coil. "Meaning?"

Maitland moved closer and began speaking in a conspiratorial whisper. "I've assumed that Cecelia became aware of our activities and left you no choice but to..." He didn't finish the thought.

He didn't have to. Jonas was well aware of the fact that Maitland, just like the Grisoms, Whitefield, Franklin Monroe and much of the rest of Charleston society, was convinced he had killed Cecelia. Their suspicions weren't without basis, he silently acknowledged. Everyone knew he had never been in love with Cecelia. Just as, if Mrs. McCafferty's gossiping was to carry any weight, everyone believed his impending marriage to Kendall was nothing more than a calculated move to redeem himself in their eyes. Word of how Kendall had saved both Colleen and her infant son had spread faster than flood waters from the Cooper River.

"Miss Butler will not be of concern to you," Jonas stated with conviction.

"But what if Whitefield presses the issue with Monroe? You know he'd do anything to get even with you for Cecelia's murder. And I'm not convinced that he believed your story about Kendall being forced to advertise for a husband. Especially after he had a look at her."

"Monroe can't do anything," Jonas insisted, though he found himself distracted by what Maitland had said. His mind immediately produced Kendall's image, as it had done time and time again since their initial meeting. She was such a unique creature. She was strong, intelligent and truly beautiful. If only she would desist from espousing her fantasies about being from another time. If only she would behave in a more fitting manner. If only he didn't want her so badly.

"WHAT'S WRONG?" Rose asked as soon as they stepped from the house.

"I don't like Mr. Maitland," she hedged, unwilling to admit to Rose that she'd been eavesdropping on the conversation between the two men.

Rose chuckled. "Few people do."

"Why are you coming, too?" she asked, taking in Rose's outlandish outfit as the woman opened a parasol against the midafternoon sun. The parasol, gown, hat, gloves and ostrich plume were all constructed in a vivid shade of fuchsia.

"Jonas asked me to."

"And you do whatever Jonas asks?" Kendall retorted, unable to keep the censure from her tone.

"Usually," Rose replied as she nodded to an older woman on the opposite side of Bay Street.

"Why?"

"He's a good man."

Kendall squinted against the sunshine, her tired eyes burning from lack of sleep. "If you're into wife murderers."

"He didn't kill Cecelia."

"How do you know that?" Kendall asked. "I've never once heard him deny it."

"Here we are," Rose announced as they came to a shop with a beautifully painted glass window. Apparently, she considered the topic of Cecelia off-limits.

The words Tanners' Dressmaking formed a golden arch above a beautifully painted gown that reminded Kendall of the fashion plates she'd seen reproduced in magazine articles.

"Oh, my God," Kendall said when she stepped inside the shop. Her startled utterance was met by two troubled sets of eyes. "Susan?"

The tall, thin redhead came forward, her dark blue eyes a mixture of curiosity and recognition. "You're Kendall," Susan said. "I knew you were coming."

"Don't start that!" Rose growled as she stepped forward and gave Kendall's arm a slight tug. "You'll have to excuse Miss Taylor. She's good with a needle and thread, but she has some strange habits and beliefs."

"I know," Kendall said. Turning back, she met Susan's eyes. "She studies numerology, tarot and pyramids."

Susan's jaw dropped open. "I saw this in the cards!" she announced excitedly. "I knew I was going to be visited by a special presence. You must be psychic, too."

"Demented," Rose grumbled. "Shelby, do something with them."

Shelby came forward and whispered something into Susan's ear. Whatever it was, it left the woman looking positively crestfallen.

"But—"

"No more," Shelby said sternly. "Miss Butler is here to have her wedding gown made, not to be lectured on the strange concepts you brought back from your trip to New Orleans. I swear, Susan, I'm sorry now that I sent you there in the first place."

"Then how did she know my name and so much about me?"

"I told her," Rose answered. Then she gave Kendall a withering look that just dared her to challenge the lie. "We'd best get on with it, ladies. The wedding is tomorrow."

If there's going to be a wedding, Kendall mouthed as she was led into a back room and assisted out of the top layers of her clothing.

"Because we have so little time, I thought it would be best if we simply altered one of the patterns," Shelby explained as she pulled out an ornate white gown with lots of lace, pearls and satin. "It shouldn't take much to fit you to this one. If you approve, that is."

"I don't really give a damn one way or another," Kendall replied.

"Oh, dear," Shelby said, sighing. Whether it was because of Kendall's language or her lack of interest wasn't clear.

Rose was grinning as she pulled one of her cigarettes from her wrist purse and placed it in the holder. "Not exactly your normal, gushing bride," she observed dryly.

Kendall stood still while Shelby and Susan tugged the heavy garment over her head and had her stand atop a wooden platform.

Kendall was shocked by her reflection in the mirror. She might not feel like a bride, but she sure looked the part. The dress was so flattering to her shape and size it almost seemed as if it had been designed with her in mind. Yards of stiff, white fabric floated out from her small waist, while the bodice lovingly hugged and accented her curves.

The three women were all admiring Kendall, complimenting her on various aspects of the gown, as well as her choice of a husband.

As if I had a choice, she thought bitterly. "Is this the same dress the first Mrs. Revell wore?"

Kendall's question caused an immediate silence in the room. Shelby and Susan looked horribly uncomfortable. Rose just looked mad.

"Am I supposed to ignore the fact that he killed his first wife?" Kendall continued, mainly to antagonize Rose. "If he holds true to form, I'll be dead by tomorrow night."

"Enough!" Rose shouted. "You don't know what you're talking about, Kendall."

"Because no one will talk to me," she insisted. "All I know is that his wife was thrown from the second-story window on their wedding night. I know someone tried to kill him, probably in retribution for Cecelia's death. If I don't marry Jonas, I'll probably be hanged by the Confederacy. Oh—" she paused from her tirade long enough to blow a stream of angry breath at a strand of hair that had fallen into her eyes "—and if I do marry Jonas, Caroline Grisom has promised to kill me. So cut me some slack if I don't feel much like a blushing bride."

"Caroline Grisom?" Shelby asked, obviously shocked.

Kendall nodded. "She stopped me on the street last night and announced that Jonas was in love with her."

Kendall saw Rose's expression change. It was a subtle change, but noticeable nonetheless. "Is that why you're so out of sorts? Because you think he's in love with that willful child, Caroline?"

"I'm out of sorts for a whole lot of reasons."

"Mr. Revell is a very handsome man," Susan said as she began marking a hem. "I'd marry him if his aura wasn't in such poor shape."

"Susan!" both Rose and Shelby warned in unison.

The woman offered a petulant look. "I just meant that he's so secretive. He's not much like the other men here in town. He's such an unusual mix of earthiness and culture. Possibly because of his background. Indian spirits and all, I guess."

Earthiness and culture. Kendall rolled the words around in her head, thinking them perfect to describe Jonas.

"I mean," Susan continued as she worked, "he's nothing like Captain Whitefield or Mr. Monroe. Not that I'd turn either one of those men down. Especially not that attractive Captain Whitefield."

"I think you're beginning to annoy Miss Butler," Shelby warned. "She didn't come here to hear your opinions of the eligible men in Charleston."

"Since the war started, there aren't that many men left in Charleston," Susan complained. "I can't wait for it to end so that we can all get back to normal."

"You've got a long wait," Kendall said under her breath. Fortunately, none of the women heard her dire prediction.

"You're so lucky," Susan said, sighing. "I bet you'd just about given up on finding a husband at your age."

"Susan!" Shelby wailed. "Apologize this instant!"

"I didn't mean any disrespect, Miss Butler," Susan said. "I guess I did sound rather impolite."

"No harm done," Kendall assured her. "But there will come a time when women decide to find themselves before they commit to marriage."

"They become lost?" Susan asked. "Did you have a premonition?"

"Good gracious!" Rose blew out an annoyed stream of bluish smoke. "Just ignore Kendall's odd use of expressions. She spent far too long in the West. We'll have to work on restoring her vocabulary to something more appropriate for correct society."

"Why don't we work on telling me some things about my future husband?" she suggested. "Like, why did he marry Cecelia if he didn't love her?"

Rose's eyes narrowed suspiciously. "Where did you hear that?"

"Jonas," she answered, failing to mention that he had been speaking to Maitland at the time and she'd been hiding in the hallway, hanging on every word.

Rose stubbed out her cigarette, her brow wrinkling as she, apparently, considered what to tell Kendall. "He needed access to Grisom's wharf to get his crop from Fairhaven to Charleston. Grisom would only agree to give a fifty-percent share to Jonas if he took his eldest daughter off his hands."

"He married Cecelia just to get access to a wharf?" Kendall repeated in amazement. "How arcane."

"How practical," Shelby interjected. "Cecelia was a bit spirited, and her father thought marrying her off to Jonas would quell her rather wild tendencies. He'd probably have done the same to poor Caroline had she not gone to live with the Monroes."

"Caroline is living with Franklin Monroe?" Kendall asked.

Shelby nodded. "And his frail mother. Mrs. Monroe hasn't been well for years. Before that, Caroline had planned to live with Jonas and Cecelia."

"Well, *poor Caroline* had enough presence of mind to threaten me. Wait . . ." Kendall's mind raced. "Was Caroline in the house the night that Cecelia died?"

"Yes," Shelby answered. "But you can't possibly think—"

"She said she was willing to kill me to have Jonas. Think she might have done her sister in for the same reason?"

"Now you really *do* sound affected," Rose announced. "Caroline idolized her elder sister. There's no way she would have harmed her."

"Then I guess that leaves Jonas as the only suspect."

"Now you sound like Mr. Monroe," Susan said. "He's been saying that all over town ever since they found her body."

"Well, he's wrong." Rose's tone and demeanor indicated that she firmly believed in Jonas's innocence.

"Friends or not, Dylan would have arrested Jonas immediately if he thought he was guilty of killing that girl."

"Did Dylan investigate?" Kendall asked.

Shelby nodded. "Of course. Jonas heard Cecelia's scream—"

"I think this is something that Jonas and Kendall should discuss among themselves," Rose cut in.

"You're right," Shelby conceded. "Dylan would not appreciate it if he knew I was even discussing such matters."

Kendall squared her shoulders and announced, "Well, I'm not sure I can marry the man without knowing the truth."

"WE'VE ALREADY been over this," Jonas said as soon as Jeffreys had finished ladling a thick soup into their bowls.

She sat across from him at the highly polished mahogany table, watching the candlelight reflected in his eyes. He looked exceptionally handsome. The crisp, white shirt contrasted nicely with his exotically dark coloring. He had left his black hair free, allowing it to brush the tops of his wide shoulders. Definitely the dark-and-dangerous type, she thought as she struggled to keep her mind focused on conversation.

"If you expect me to go through with this wedding, then you're going to have to be a bit more forthcoming about yourself."

"There's nothing about me you need to know, other than the fact that I am fully capable of seeing to your needs."

"You don't know me, so what makes you think you can possibly know my needs?"

Jonas laid his spoon next to his bowl, rested his elbows on the table and steepled his fingers. His eyes met hers. "Like other women, I assume you require the basic comforts."

"I'm sure I can get food, clothing and shelter from the local parish," Kendall commented rather loudly. "I know you got a wharf privilege out of your first marriage. What do you expect to get out of this one?"

She felt a small measure of satisfaction in that brief instant when surprise registered in his eyes.

He recovered quickly and replied, "After last night, I would think the answer to that was obvious."

It was Kendall's turn to be surprised. "You're marrying me for sex?"

He closed his eyes, obviously unhappy with her frankness. When he looked at her again, his expression seemed stiff. "It is a common practice between married couples."

"Not *this* married couple," Kendall assured him.

"I'm afraid that is nonnegotiable," Jonas told her. "I've had one unconsummated marriage. I don't intend to suffer another."

"You mean you and Cecelia never..."

"Of course not," he answered primly.

"But I heard she was pretty wild. If you kissed her the way you kiss me, I don't—" Kendall snapped her mouth closed, realizing too late what she had revealed.

Her meaning wasn't lost on Jonas, and he acted almost instantaneously. He rounded the table and gathered her against him, immediately locking his mouth on hers. He felt her reluctance, but not as strongly as he felt her response. Kendall's initial rigidness soon gave way to compliance as he teased her lips apart.

Jonas felt as if his body would explode. His desire for this woman was strong, almost overpowering in its intensity. What was worse—or better—was the way she moved against him. He'd never had a woman respond so honestly, so completely. It was as if she wasn't the least bit ashamed of her desires, and that only added fuel to his own.

He wanted to have her right then and there. Nothing seemed as important as his fierce need to feel her beneath him. He wondered if her skin was as silky as her hair. He wondered if she would make love with the same abandon she displayed whenever she returned his kisses. He wondered if he could wait another twelve hours.

"You're driving me mad, Kendall," he said against her mouth.

"Then don't do this" came her breathy reply.

He held her against him for a few minutes, until he could release her without suffering the embarrassment of revealing the obvious physical reaction straining his trousers.

"I think you do that just so we can't have a conversation," she said when he held her chair out for her.

"Perhaps." His reasons for kissing her were too complex. He was only sorry that Kendall wasn't the kind of woman to be kissed speechless.

"What exactly are you and Maitland into?" she asked as soon as he had taken his seat and lifted his spoon.

"I don't want to talk about Maitland."

"And you didn't want to talk about me to him," she said. "But I'm not as easily put off as he was."

Jonas felt his grip tighten on the utensil. "You were listening to my conversation?"

"Yes," she said without apology.

"That will prove a very dangerous habit, Kendall. Don't do it again."

"Then talk to me," she pleaded. "Part of me still believes that I'm dreaming and I'll wake up and be safe in my own bed. Another part of me is starting to think all this is real."

"I am real, Kendall."

"Not that," she said quietly. "My being here goes against everything I ever learned. People don't just zip into another time. But so far, I can't seem to figure out how or why I'm here."

"You're here to marry me, since your family has fallen on hard times and cannot possibly afford to continue with your maintenance."

"C'mon, Jonas. That pile of garbage was all in Rose's imagination."

Her expression was a melding of frustration, fear and confusion, and it seemed to inspire all of his protective instincts. It also reminded him that she was delusional enough to be considered for commitment. But then, he'd seen what she had done with Colleen. Was it possible?

"It worked, though," he reminded her. "It kept you from being arrested."

"Why do you care if I get arrested?" she countered, her blue eyes flashing with challenge. "Why would you go to such lengths, when all you had to do was hand me over to Captain Whitefield?"

"Because Whitefield would have you killed."

She took in a breath and exhaled slowly. "As I recall, you were ready to kill me on a couple of different occasions."

"So long as you do as I say, you needn't worry that any harm will come to you."

"Obeying has never been one of my strong suits," she told him with a small smile that seemed to return some of the sparkle to her eyes.

"No, I don't imagine it has been."

"What if I just left," she suggested. "Give me back the locket, and I'll go someplace else until I can figure out how to get back to my own time."

"I can't let you do that," Jonas said with a sigh.

"Why? I know you don't really want to marry me, so it isn't that."

Jonas got up, checked that none of the servants were by the door, then returned to his seat. "I do want to marry you," he said.

"Bull—"

"I would rather marry you than turn you over to Maitland, who would surely kill you. Since you saved my life, I think it only fitting that I return the favor."

"A simple thank-you was enough," she told him. "Please, Jonas, just let me leave."

"I can't, Kendall," he said as his eyes locked with hers. "I would be risking myself and countless others. You know too much."

"I don't know anything! That's why we're having this conversation."

He nodded once and said, "True. I suppose if you're going to be convinced that we have no alternatives, I should tell you what I can."

"Finally."

"I'm a spy, Kendall."

She stared for a moment before she said, "Obviously, you feel a strong allegiance to The Cause and all, but the Union army will win, and since the Confederacy wasn't real good at cryptology, most all the spies are caught and—"

"You misunderstand, Kendall. I'm working to preserve the Union."

Chapter Eight

"The Union?" she repeated. "You're a Northern spy?"

"Hush!" he said in a softly commanding tone. "Now I hope you can appreciate that I cannot permit you to leave here under any circumstances."

She glared at him. "You told me that just so you'd have something to hold me here. That was a cheap trick, Revell."

"You're the one who seemed to need convincing."

"But you didn't have to admit that," she said. "And Maitland works with you, so that explains why he's in such a hurry to see me dead. He's afraid I'll give you away."

"Precisely."

"That's why he identified me to Captain White-field. He was hoping he could get the Confederate army to do his dirty work for him."

"Right again."

"And you think he's the one who shot you that night?"

Jonas stroked the shadow of a beard on his jawline. "I considered that."

"And he denied it."

"Maitland needs me. I'm his only source of information regarding shipments out of England."

"Then he probably wouldn't shoot you," Kendall reasoned.

"But he might have been aiming for you."

A shiver danced along her spine. "I've never been this unpopular in my life," she observed dryly.

"If it makes you feel any better, I don't think Maitland is the responsible party."

"Unless Caroline is psychic and knew I was here, that means you had to be the target that night."

He nodded as casually as if she had just told him the correct time.

"How many people know you're a spy?"

"Three, including you."

"I didn't shoot you."

"I know. Nor did Maitland. And the third person couldn't possibly have anything to do with it."

"Who is the third person?"

Jonas shook his head, the candlelight picking up the blue-black highlights in his hair. "Sorry, Kendall."

"I don't like secrets," she informed him stiffly. "Especially the kind that can get me killed. If I know who the third person is, I can keep my eyes open."

"That isn't necessary. The person is no threat to either of us."

He said it with such finality that she knew he would remove his own spleen with an oyster fork before he would reveal the name.

"Then I guess that means you've decided that who-ever shot you was trying to get even for Cecelia's murder."

His lips pulled into a tight line before he nodded. "It only stands to reason."

Kendall met and held his eyes, staring deep into their gray pools. "Rose, Shelby and Susan all believe you didn't kill her."

"I know."

Her gaze didn't falter. "If you want me to marry you, Jonas, I have to know it, too."

His expression never wavered as he said, "I didn't kill her."

SHE WAS UP EARLY the next morning, trying to decide what to do. *How far can I get on foot when the coun-tryside is swarming with trigger-happy soldiers enthu-siastic for battle?* she wondered as she hugged the edges of her robe tightly together. As she stood next to the window, a flash of black drew her eyes to the street below. "Where is he going?" she muttered, recogniz-ing Jonas by his unmistakable swagger.

If Jonas is out, I might just be able to find out what he did with my locket, she thought. Wasting no time, Kendall slipped from her room and padded barefoot across the hall. Mindful of the servants, she eased open the door.

The room seemed to suit what she knew about Jonas. The furniture was huge and masculine, constructed in dark, rich woods with deep carvings. The walls were adorned with an eclectic mixture of heavily framed oils and interesting sand paintings.

Knowing she didn't have much time, she moved first to the huge dresser. The drawer squeaked loudly as she pulled it open. She reached in and felt beneath the clothing. Nothing. She did the same with each of the eight drawers. Nothing.

Moving to the wardrobe, she pulled open the doors and found another set of drawers beneath the neatly hung collection of Jonas's clothing. She was rifling the third drawer when she heard a noise behind her.

"Jonas?"

"Looking for something?"

Kendall felt her face flame as she slammed closed the doors. "I was looking for the locket."

He didn't appear angry. In fact, he acted as if he'd been expecting that very answer.

"I have it," he told her easily as he shrugged out of his topcoat and tossed it onto the high bed, avoiding the carefully laid out suit and shirt.

It was only then that she realized they were the clothes he intended to wear to the wedding. It was a sobering thought.

"None of this will be necessary if you'll just give me back the locket," she told him. "I got here when I put it on. It has to be the key to getting me back to where I belong."

Jonas leaned against the doorjamb, crossing one booted ankle over the other. A slightly tolerant look softened his features.

"If I let you try on the locket once again, and it doesn't do what you expect, what then?" he taunted.

"Then . . ." Kendall paused, trying to think of the right words to make him turn over the necklace. "Then I promise I'll be completely cooperative with the wedding."

"Not quite good enough." He sighed.

"Then what?"

"You'll be completely cooperative with the marriage," he answered. His gray eyes darkened slightly, leaving nothing to her imagination.

"Jonas!" she cried.

"Those are the terms," he said with a shrug. Then, as if she were some sort of trained animal, he reached into his pocket and produced the locket, allowing it to dangle invitingly from his forefinger. "Well?"

"You're making a bad bargain," she told him as she walked over and snatched the necklace from him, ignoring his smug expression in the process.

"I doubt it," he observed as his eyes roamed over the thin fabric of her nightgown where her robe had fallen open.

Kendall gave him a reproachful glare. "We aren't married yet," she snapped as she belted her robe and then slowly lifted the locket and placed it over her head. Closing her eyes, she waited.

"You're still here."

"I know that!" she practically shouted. "I must have done something differently." Rubbing her temples, Kendall tried to think back to her lunch on the veranda. "That's it—I'm in the wrong place."

Nearly shoving Jonas out of the way, Kendall raced down the stairs and went out onto the side porch. Jonas was right on her heels.

"It isn't proper for you to be out here in your current state of undress."

"Hopefully, I won't be out here long," she assured him as she took the locket off, rubbed it between her palms, then slipped it back around her neck.

"Enough of this foolishness," Jonas said against her ear before he lifted her into his arms and carried her back inside.

"You didn't give it enough time," Kendall complained when he gently set her in the middle of the parlor floor.

Jonas stood over her, his palm held out. "I'll take the locket now, and you will go upstairs and begin preparations for our wedding."

"But, Jonas!"

"We had a deal," he reminded her with that sexy half smile that produced that even sexier dimple. "I honored my part of the bargain. Now you'll honor yours."

Gritting her teeth, Kendall removed the necklace and placed it in his palm. The instant she did, his large hand closed on hers. He brought it to his lips, and while his eyes fixed on her, Jonas placed a light kiss on each of her knuckles.

Obviously, he thought he could seduce away her anger. He thought the mere touch of his mouth would be enough to make her forget that she was trapped. If the weakness in her knees was any indication, he was absolutely right.

"SIT STILL so I can get this into your hair properlike," Mrs. McCafferty chided.

"Sorry," Kendall muttered. "I guess I'm just nervous," she admitted just as she felt herself being gored by a hairpin. "Ouch!"

"Sorry. I'm just trying to make sure they don't show in your light hair." Mrs. McCafferty delivered a few more jabs before she seemed satisfied that the veil was securely fastened. Only then did she allow Kendall to turn toward the mirror. "His Lordship will be mighty pleased," she said with an assured grin. "My Colleen sends her best."

"How is she feeling?" Kendall asked. She wished she had a curling iron so that she might do something just a bit more creative with her hair. However, considering her limited options, she had settled on allowing Mrs. McCafferty to create ringlets. Feeling a little too much like an overaged Shirley Temple, Kendall took the comb and began working with the curls left free of the veil.

"She's feeling stronger every day," Mrs. McCafferty declared, beaming. "The baby is as healthy as a horse. Only, that idiot she married isn't here, so she won't give the boy a proper name. See here," she began. "What are you trying to do?"

"I'll feel more like myself this way," Kendall explained as she teased the curls into soft tendrils that framed her face.

"I see your point," Mrs. McCafferty said as she stood behind her, watching the technique. "Hurry now. It's a long ride out to Stella Maris."

"Isn't there a Catholic church here in town?" Kendall asked, not looking forward to a long carriage ride that would probably ruin her beautiful gown.

"His Lordship wants the service to take place there so that folks can gather at Fairhaven afterward."

There was something about the way she wasn't meeting Kendall's eyes that made Kendall suspicious of the older woman. "What's the real reason?" she pressed.

"The priest who married him and the first missus refused to perform the ceremony."

Kendall nodded as she digested the information. She could hardly blame the man. He probably thought Jonas had murdered his wife, and didn't want any part in a possible repeat of history.

Shelby, Susan and Rose all arrived to help Kendall dress and to escort her to the church. "Was this Jonas's idea?" she asked Shelby as she worked on the rows of buttons that fastened the sleeves. "Was he afraid I wouldn't go?"

Shelby's smile was polite. "I think he simply wanted to make sure that you got into this dress. He's downstairs with Dylan. I'd be happy to ask him."

"Maybe Dylan will talk him out of this," Kendall said with a sigh.

"I was told you had had a change of heart," Rose said from where she sat in front of the dry sink, primping her pile of hair. "Jonas told me you were ready and willing."

"I'm doing it, right?" Kendall remarked. "I'm trussed up in more corsets and cloth than a mummy."

"Have you ever seen a mummy?" Susan asked excitedly. "I mean, a real one? I did. It was on exhibit when I was in Boston buying fabric for—"

"Hush up," Rose admonished. "I swear, your infernal chatter could drive a person to drink."

"All done," Shelby announced.

She spun Kendall around to observe the overall effect. Her smile told Kendall more than any mirror could.

"You look stunning."

"I feel silly," Kendall grumbled. "This has all happened so fast that I don't even have anyone to walk me down the aisle."

"Dylan's going to do that before he stands up for Jonas," Shelby explained.

"And Shelby will act as your matron of honor," Rose stated. When Kendall's face must have registered surprise, Rose went on. "According to your betrothed, I'm a bit—I believe his word was 'flamboyant'—to stand before God and his followers."

One look at Rose's attire attested to the truth of Jonas's concerns. Her gown was a bright russet, bordering on orange. Her hat, though much more simple than the highly decorated ones she favored, sported a single stuffed blue jay, pinned to one side.

Shelby, on the other hand, was dressed in a pale-blue silk that complemented her dark coloring and very nearly matched her blue eyes. She looked elegant in the simple gown. Kendall couldn't have asked for more, and she couldn't help but think that had this been happening in her own time, she would have asked these same people to perform these same duties.

KENDALL WAS IN the second carriage of the caravan leaving the city. Given the fact that Jonas had so many enemies, she was stunned to realize how many guests would be in attendance.

"Who are all these people?" she asked Shelby.

"Everyone who is anyone will be here. This is an event."

"Freak show," she muttered. "But I was under the impression that all these people think Jonas is a murderer."

"But they'll gladly put those thoughts aside for the day, if it means attending a party at Fairhaven," Rose said. "Only a fool would miss an event at Fairhaven."

Kendall hadn't given the plantation much thought until then. Of course, she had more than an hour of a bumpy, jerky carriage ride to think. Fairhaven seemed somehow familiar. Maybe it was one of the plantations frequented by tourists. Lord, what would Jonas think if he knew his home would someday be open to the public for a few dollars a clip?

Kendall and Shelby were ushered into an anteroom of the church. Her anxiety level was almost as high as the ceilings of the masonry building. She jumped when she heard a distant crash. "Great," she said. "It's going to rain."

"That isn't thunder," Shelby said softly. "That's cannon fire."

"Rain would be better," Kendall conceded with a wry smile.

"Don't worry. Dylan checked and the ships are way up the Ashley River. They can't possibly get here to spoil things for you."

Kendall looked at the taller woman for some time, until it became apparent that she was making Shelby nervous. "I'm sorry, it's just that I *do* know you."

Shelby's smile faltered.

"I know all about you and Dylan and Chad and Cassidy."

Shelby's smile fell away completely.

"I know that Chad was kidnapped and I know how you anguished to get him back. I know that Cassidy wasn't planned and that Dylan is one of six children. I know you were adopted by a loving stepfather. I know—"

Kendall's words were cut off by the sudden appearance of Rose, slipping through the door. Rose looked from woman to woman before turning impatient green eyes on Kendall. "What did you say to Shelby? You haven't decided to make a run for it, have you?"

"It isn't that," Shelby said in a raspy whisper.

"Then what? You aren't ill, are you?" Rose asked, going to the other woman's side. "You're not expecting again so soon, are you?"

Shelby looked at Rose and Kendall, trying to decide whether or not to remain silent.

"Have you told her anything about me?" Shelby asked.

Rose shook her head and shot Kendall a withering look.

"But she knows *everything*," Shelby said. "She knows about the Hunnicutts. No one except you and Dylan know that I was a foundling."

Chapter Nine

It could have been called the wedding of the stone statues, Kendall thought as the priest proclaimed them man and wife. Her conversation with Shelby had rendered the woman stiff and robotlike. Rose had glared at her as she made her way up the aisle in front of a gaping capacity crowd. When Dylan had passed her to her groom at the altar, Jonas had accepted her with the enthusiasm of a man accepting a sack of mealy flour.

She was drawn from her musings by the feel of Jonas raising her veil. Peering up at him through her lashes, she noted, sadly, that there was no joy, no happiness, no nothing in those gray eyes. Jonas appeared more distant than she had ever seen him.

The kiss he offered wasn't like any of the previous ones they had shared. This was a cold, unfeeling touch of his mouth to hers, which inspired none of the usual heat or passion. When they turned to walk back down the aisle, Kendall was nearly paralyzed by the unexpected sight of Harris Grisom and his sobbing daughter, Caroline, among the attendees.

"I'll bet he didn't spring for a wedding present," Kendall whispered through her fake smile.

"I'm sure he's only here to make certain we went through with it."

When they entered the waiting carriage, Kendall was sorry to see that Jonas's mood hadn't improved. Tossing her bundle of tied flowers on the seat next to her, she stared at her husband.

Husband. The word made her shiver.

"Are you cold?"

"With the frosty treatment you're giving me, how could I not be cold?" she asked smartly.

Jonas had the decency to appear contrite. "When I saw the look on Shelby's face as she came down the aisle, I was almost certain you had made a run for it."

Tilting her head back to study him, Kendall found herself smiling. "You were as nervous as I was."

"Worse," he said on an expelled breath. "I decided that the only thing that could make Shelby Tanner look so stricken was if you had left her the grim task of announcing your refusal to go through with the wedding."

"I'm afraid I did say something that upset her," Kendall admitted with some regret.

"Shelby is one of the finest women I know," Jonas lectured. "I would insist that you would refrain from upsetting her in the future."

"Insist?" Kendall repeated. "As in 'order'?"

Jonas grinned sheepishly. "You did just promise to obey."

"I lied."

His laughter echoed in the small compartment as they set out for Fairhaven. Kendall twisted the slender gold band on her finger until she caught her first sight of the plantation. "This is Fairhaven?" she asked.

"Yes," he answered as his brows drew together in apparent response to her astonished tone.

Kendall recognized the Georgian-Palladian architecture instantly. What she didn't recognize was the condition. Jonas would be heartbroken to learn that in the 1990s, this beautiful home was little more than a pile of rubble. Nothing but the exterior walls remained of what, she now could see, were beautiful, geometric gardens.

"Welcome home, sir" a young black boy said with his eyes downcast as he hurriedly positioned a footstool. "And congratulations to you both."

"Thank you, Simon. Is everything in readiness?"

"Yes, sir."

Jonas got out first, then extended his hand to Kendall, assisting her with the yards of fabric that comprised her skirt. The scent of late-blooming flowers mingled with the faint smell of a cooking fire. Ribbons and bows decorated the recessed, two-story portico. Several servants milled at the front door.

"Are they slaves?" Kendall asked after giving Jonas's arm a jerk and getting him to dip his head so that she could ask the question discreetly.

"Legally or morally?"

"Either...both. I know Mrs. McCafferty is some sort of indentured servant, but I never thought about the possibility of you owning other human beings."

Jonas led her behind one of the live oaks, trying to make it look as though they might be stealing a passionate moment together.

"If you say something like that to the wrong person, you will be hanged. Do you understand?"

"But, Jonas. I don't know if I can stand the idea of you being a slave owner."

"Give it time, Kendall."

Time was one thing she didn't have. No sooner had they emerged from behind the tree than the carriages began to arrive.

Jonas ushered her inside after brief introductions to the happy group who didn't appear at all bothered by the circumstances of their existence. If she thought the Rose Tattoo was impressive, Fairhaven put it to shame. The twenty-five rooms were filled with carved woodwork, marble fireplaces and furniture that was surely museum quality. Music from a talented ensemble wafted through the house, as did the din of conversation.

"I'LL CALL HATTIE if you'd like to freshen up before the party," Jonas said as he adjusted his tie in the mirror.

"I'm fine," she told him as she stood stiffly gripping her bouquet.

Seeing her like that, Jonas took a deep breath before closing the bedroom door. "It's too complicated to explain to you now," he said. "If it will salve your conscience, I've never mistreated anyone in my life."

"There's still a principle involved here," she argued.

"But as you so often remind me, dear wife, this is my time, my rules."

He saw the flicker of hope in her eyes. "Does that mean you finally believe what I've been telling you?"

"I'm trying very hard to accept your word," he said as he moved to stand in front of her. "I would only ask that you afford me the same courtesy."

When she lowered her eyes, Jonas took her chin between his thumb and finger, forcing her to meet his gaze. "Now, unless you want all our guests to assume we couldn't wait until this evening, I suggest we go downstairs."

"Wait," she said with an urgency he hadn't expected.

He felt her small hand grip his forearm. "Yes?"

"May I ask a favor?"

"Of course."

"I felt a little cheated at the church. I'd really like it if you'd kiss me as if you meant it."

"As you wish," he managed to get out before he pulled her into his embrace. His mouth moved over hers with a power and possessiveness he'd never felt before. Her body rippled in his arms, almost making him regret starting something he knew they couldn't finish. It didn't matter. Nothing seemed to matter at that moment except the feel of her small body molded to his. His body reacted quickly and predictably, and he moaned into her opened mouth. He didn't know what kind of power she had. Maybe she *was* some sort of vision from the future. At least that would explain why kissing her, touching her, was like nothing he'd ever experienced in his lifetime.

When she moved against him, Jonas knew he no longer cared if the king himself was waiting below. His hand slid from her back down to her small waist. She responded to his touch, pressing herself against him so intimately that his self-control teetered on the brink.

"Sorry."

Dylan's voice broke through his clouded thoughts.

Kendall jumped away from Jonas as if he were on fire. He was, but then, if the flush on her cheeks was any indication, so was she.

"I take it we're being missed?" Jonas asked as he raked his slightly trembling hand through his hair and retied the rawhide strap.

"I can probably think up some excuse if you want..." Dylan offered.

"We'll come down," he heard Kendall insist.

Her apparent desire to get away from him didn't do much for his ego.

With his wife at his side, Jonas descended the carved staircase, noting with wry amusement that nearly the entire group was eyeing them with blatant curiosity, although the true blue bloods hid their interest behind quickly moving fans or gloved hands.

Jonas was extremely impressed by the way Kendall handled the awkward situation. Instead of hiding behind him as most any other woman would have done, she lifted her chin proudly and donned her brightest smile.

He found Rose in the crowd, and was relieved when he got her private nod of approval. Shelby's smile was genuine, though her eyes still looked troubled. He made a mental note to speak to Kendall again, wondering what on earth she could have said to upset Shelby.

"Hungry?" he inquired against her ear as he handed her a glass of champagne.

The look she gave him in reply was secretive and intimate, and conveyed her answer far better than a simple word. He smiled down at her, feeling oddly pleased by the anticipation and hunger he saw in her eyes.

"It would be considered scandalous if we didn't at least sit for photographs and manage at least one dance," he murmured against her hair. "I'll tell the photographer we're ready."

Jonas couldn't recall the last time he had barked so many orders in such a short span of time. With his baser instincts guiding him, he managed to speed the process of the celebration, much to the apparent disappointment of most of the guests. Only Rose, Dylan and Shelby seemed to understand his need for haste, and they did everything to see that the house was emptied just after nightfall.

"I didn't think they would ever leave," Jonas said as he stood at Kendall's side, his fingers splayed at the center of her back.

"I'm surprised they stayed as long as they did, given your rather inhospitable behavior."

Jonas took her hand in his, leading her toward the staircase. He felt a slight resistance and found it puzzling. "This was part of our bargain," he reminded her, instantly sorry when he felt her jerk her hand out of his grasp.

"I don't need to be reminded," she told him stiffly before moving past him to climb the stairs.

Jonas followed, wondering what had happened. All during the afternoon she had smiled, danced and seemed genuinely resigned to their fate, almost happy. Now he felt he was watching a complete stranger. Her sudden frigidness brought back another reminder of his first ill-fated wedding day. Cecelia had behaved similarly. On that occasion, he had remained downstairs, thinking some privacy would calm her nerves. Well, Kendall wasn't Cecelia. He hadn't wanted Cecelia. He wanted Kendall and he had no intention of giving her time to think of a good excuse to deny him what was his by rights.

Taking the stairs two at a time, Jonas found the bedroom door closed. He didn't hesitate. He burst through the door—and then froze.

Kendall was by the fire, standing next to the mound of fabric that had been her dress. The generous amount of bosom he could see above the lacy edges of her corset made his mouth go dry. She was staring at him, her eyes in direct contradiction to her posture. That flicker of uncertainty didn't fit with the way she seemed not to care that he could see virtually all of her through the thin fabric of her undergarments.

"I'm sure I'm not the first woman you've seen in a state of partial undress," she said, though the lightness seemed forced.

"But..."

She paused. The wringing of her hands was the only outward sign of nervousness he could detect.

"I think we need to have a little talk before we have biblical knowledge of each other."

"Talk?" Jonas repeated in amazement. He was already ripping off his coat and tie. He took two strides forward, but the look in her wide eyes halted him. Closing his eyes, he mentally wished for control. "Talk, Kendall, but do be quick about it."

"I have to tell you something. It might change your mind about doing this."

"You're welcome to try."

She smiled at his oft-used expression and he felt himself relax slightly. He wondered if she knew there was nothing she could say that could possibly quell his desire. The only thing that would satisfy him now was having her, completely.

"I haven't done this before," she said on a rush of breath.

Allowing his head to fall to the side, he studied her for a moment. "I didn't assume that you had, since you've never been married."

Her smile widened. "In my time, marriage isn't necessary. It is considered acceptable to most people for couples to have sex without any commitment. In fact, I'm considered the oddity."

"How can that be?"

Kendall shrugged. "I could tell you all about the Sexual Revolution and the Age of Aquarius, but the easiest explanation is to simply say that a lot people decided sex was good for more than just procreation."

Jonas went to the edge of the bed and sat down. His eyes were still fixed on her as he tried to remind himself that if he challenged her delusions at this point, it might just cost him his wedding night. "Why are you an oddity then?"

"Because I'm twenty-seven years old and still a virgin. It isn't considered normal to wait this long."

"Why did you?"

"I was really committed to getting through school, and I guess enough of what I was taught in Catholic school kicked in. Then, by the time I was in medical school and getting pretty curious, AIDS came along."

"The men in your time require aid in order to make love?"

She laughed. "Not aid, A-I-D-S. It's a terrible disease that is often transmitted through sexual contact. Like syphilis."

"Kendall," he groaned, raking his hands through his hair, then removing his tie. "It isn't appropriate for us to discuss things such as this."

"That's one of the things that set off the Sexual Revolution," she said as she came and sat next to him on the bed. "You thought I had changed my mind, but I haven't. In fact, I'm so curious I've had to struggle to keep from creeping into your room at night, ever since that first time you kissed me."

"I think we've talked long enough," he said quietly.

He turned and eased down on top of her, grinning at the mixture of hunger and embarrassment on her face.

Bracing his weight with one arm, he rolled her onto her side so that he could untie the miles of lacing that held her corset together. All the while he watched her expression, watched as she reacted as the garment loosened, until he was able to peel it away.

"You're incredible," he whispered as his eyes took in her nakedness. Next, his hands found the ties for her petticoats, and he made quick work of them, until she lay next to him, beautifully exposed.

"You're dressed," she said as her slightly trembling fingers reached for the buttons of his shirt.

Kendall was amazingly adept at removing his clothing, and when she looked up at him, his observation must have registered, for she said, "I've undressed hundreds of men as part of my training, Jonas. Most of the time, especially when I was on my ER rotation, we cut the clothes off. You don't need to worry—I won't faint dead at the sight of you in your birthday suit."

"Birthday suit?"

He was sorry he had even asked the question. With her hands on his body, he didn't care if she wanted to tell tall tales about fairies and leprechauns. He didn't wait for her to answer. He simply pushed her down on the mattress and began to kiss her with an intensity that bordered on the savage. He just couldn't seem to get close enough to her.

Slipping one hand beneath her small hip, he lifted her against him, marveling at the small sound that rumbled in her throat.

Jonas raised his head, waiting the few reassuring seconds for her to reach for him and pull him back to her. It left no doubt in his mind that she wanted this as much as he did. That knowledge brought with it a complete loss of control.

Using one thigh, he parted her legs and arched up with the intention of burying himself inside of her.

Kendall had a different idea. Placing her hands on his shoulders, she pushed him on his back, rolling with him until she lay on top of him. Her floral-scented hair fell across his face. Grabbing her hair and tossing it out of the way with one hand, she cupped his face with the other.

Looking directly into his eyes, she said, "We're going to do this my way, okay?"

At that instant, Jonas would have agreed to anything. He nodded mutely as Kendall moved to the side and began to touch him everywhere. He brought his forearm up to cover his eyes as he grimaced and waged war with his self-control. She was driving him mad with her feathery touches.

"Kendall." He whispered her name like a prayer.

"Yes?"

"I'm not sure I can tolerate much more of this."

"Then participate."

Dropping his arm, he looked at her flushed face and sensual smile, then dipped his head and took the peak of her nipple into his mouth. She arched against him like a cat; her fingers immediately wound through his hair, holding him to her.

His hands weren't idle, either. She dug her nails gently into his scalp as he explored her, cherishing every little pleasurable sound she made. When he dragged his opened mouth over the supple curve of her throat, Kendall cried out with total abandon, and he knew the time was right.

He tried to place her on her back, yet she resisted. When he lifted his head, he found her expression wild, her body covered in a sheen of perspiration.

"Let me," she managed hoarsely.

Jonas threw his head back against the pillow, wondering what she planned next. He wasn't sure he could withstand satisfying her curiosity any longer. His body was so tense, so taut, he wasn't even sure he could last the course.

Kendall lifted her shapely leg over his body; then, straddling him, gently and slowly controlled their joining. It was amazing—unheard of, even—to watch her, but he did, his eyes never leaving her face. He flinched only once when he saw a flicker of discomfort mar her features, but that seemed to pass quickly as they fell into an age-old rhythm.

His whole body became as taut as a bow as he watched her mouth fall open and her breathing become shallow. He feared he was hurting her, but she felt so good that he was powerless to stop.

Kendall reared back suddenly, then he felt her body shudder and go limp. She moaned softly, which only added to his confusion.

"Kendall?"

Her head rested in the hollow of his shoulder, her breathing still uneven as she resumed the slow, tantalizing movement of her hips. Confusion was forgotten as he focused on the carnal pleasure of her movements. It didn't take much for her to send him over the edge. At the moment of his release, Jonas placed his hands on her hips and held her tightly as he exploded inside of her.

"Kendall?"

"Mmmm," she purred as she stretched her body against his. He had already suffered through having her sleep next to him completely naked. Now he was apparently supposed to endure the torture of having her move.

"Kendall," he said more forcefully.

Lifting her head, she shifted into a half-sitting position, not bothering to cover herself in the process. Jonas made a valiant attempt to keep from looking. He failed.

"Have you no shame?" he asked when he had looked his fill.

He imagined her smile matched his own. "Apparently not," she said. Only then did she lift the edge of the blanket to a more modest level. "But then again, I doubt there's much of me you haven't already seen, so what's the point?"

"The point is," he said as he placed a kiss on her cheek, "we have to get back to town. Which won't happen if you insist on flaunting your...charms in front of me."

"Town?" she wailed. "Why do we have to go back? We just got married. We're supposed to be on our honeymoon." She reached out and grabbed his arm as he attempted to get out of bed. "We're supposed to stay in bed for a week, making mad, passionate love until we go blind."

"Good Lord, woman!" Jonas cried as he shrugged out of bed, shaking his head as he chuckled.

Stepping into his trousers, he was surprised when he didn't hear any further comments from Kendall. Pouting wasn't her style. He turned to see her looking stricken. "What did I say?"

She lifted her eyes and he was stunned to find them moist with unshed tears. He was even more stunned by the way it made him feel. "What?" he repeated, moving next to her and pulling her into the circle of his arms.

"I guess it was pretty disappointing then, huh?"

"What?"

He felt her shake her head. "Don't play dumb, Jonas. All you have to do is say I wasn't what you expected. You don't need to make up reasons not to—"

"You really have lost touch, haven't you?" he asked, giving her a little shake. "I would love nothing better than to stay in bed with you for that week you were discussing, but I'm afraid we simply can't."

"Why not?"

"Because the Union ships patrol the river and they delight in firing upon the houses along their banks. It simply isn't safe for us to stay here."

Jonas lifted her face and brushed a few strands of hair out of her eyes. "If you doubt my honesty, Kendall, explain this." He smiled smugly when she gave a little gasp as soon as he had placed her hand over a certain portion of his anatomy that gave testimony to his words. "We'll leave after breakfast."

KENDALL DECLINED the assistance of the young girl sent up to help her dress. The damned corset could just stay loosely tied.

Joining Jonas in the airy, stunning breakfast room gave her a new appreciation for Southern charm and beauty. Nothing she had ever been taught as a child could have prepared her for the reality of this. Everything was perfect, especially Jonas's look as she entered the room.

Ever the gentleman, he rose and saw her seated.

"Thank you," she said, feeling suddenly awkward. It was strange, but the intimacy they had shared had drastically changed the way she thought of him.

"Coffee?" The question came from the same young girl who had been dispatched to assist Kendall. She spoke to Jonas, keeping her eyes fixed on some distant point.

"Yes, and for Lady Revell, as well."

Lady Revell, Kendall repeated in her brain. As soon as the girl left, she turned to Jonas and said, "I prefer *Dr.* Revell."

He gave her one of his tolerant smiles and she felt herself growing annoyed. "Don't patronize me, Jonas. Either you accept what I am or let me go."

Leaning back in his chair, he regarded her for several long moments over the rim of his coffee cup. "You don't ask for much, do you, Kendall?"

"Actually," she began with a loud sigh, "I have been meaning to ask you about something else."

One dark brow raised and a smile curved the corners of his mouth.

"I've been thinking about why the locket didn't take me back to my time."

"I believe we have already dispensed with that bit of folly."

She glared at him. "It isn't folly—something you will learn in about ten days when the fire breaks out. I'm willing to wait until then for you to eat crow. Now, back to the locket."

"Must we?"

"Yes," she told him firmly. "Maybe I can't return to my time because I have some sort of purpose to fulfill here."

"Christlike delusions are sinful."

"Nothing quite so lofty," she retorted. "I was thinking more along the lines of proving that you didn't kill your wife."

"You are my wife."

Kendall felt her cheeks warm and she averted her eyes for a moment. "Your first wife. Maybe if I can clear your name, I can get back to my time."

"This is all very fascinating, Kendall, but I think you're taking this fantasy a bit too far."

"It isn't a fantasy. I don't belong here."

"After last night, I would tend to disagree with you."

Her blush deepened. "I can't stay in a time I don't belong just for great sex."

"Great?"

Her patience was wearing thin. "Damn it, Jonas! I'm serious! All I want is a chance to prove that you didn't kill your wife."

His expression grew heavy, as if he would be sorry to see her out of his life. She knew she was reading more into it than was there. The whole notion that Jonas had actually developed feelings for her in such a short time was ludicrous. As ludicrous as the thought that she would miss him when, and if, she could get home. Suddenly her mind flashed a kaleidoscope of memories—his laughter, his dimple, their wedding, the incredible way they had made love.

"What exactly do you want, Kendall?"

"I want to perform an autopsy on Cecelia's remains."

Chapter Ten

"How disgusting," Rose said. "I hope you told her no."

"Of course," Jonas answered.

Kendall sat at the table fuming. It was bad enough that Jonas had flatly refused even to consider allowing her to perform an autopsy on Cecelia. But the fact that he had brought it up as dinner conversation that evening only made matters worse. Hell, she was still miffed to discover that on their first full day as man and wife, he had invited the Tanners and Rose for dinner.

"Jonas doesn't believe any of what I've been telling him," Kendall said with a saccharine smile. She noticed Shelby's expression grow solemn. "You know better, though, don't you, Shelby?"

"Kendall," Jonas warned.

There was a silence as Dylan, Jonas and Rose all watched as the normally poised Shelby appeared to struggle with an appropriate response.

"I told you I would not tolerate you upsetting Shelby," Jonas growled.

His eyes were dark and stormy, but Kendall was determined. "Careful, Jonas. You really shouldn't look at your wife with murder in your eyes. People will talk—again."

Her barb was a direct hit. He looked as though he would gladly get out of his chair and strangle her. His hands balled into tight fists and a vein in the side of his neck was bulging.

"Go upstairs," he said.

"Go to hell," she retorted with a sweet smile. "I warned you I wasn't too good at obeying."

"That's it!" Jonas said as he began to rise.

"Wait," Shelby interjected. "Please, there's no reason for the two of you to fight on my account."

"I'll bet they'll fight on anyone's account," Rose said, smugly leaning back as if enjoying a performance. "They're two headstrong people."

"Jonas," Shelby began. "Kendall does seem to have an uncanny knowledge where we are all concerned."

Kendall watched as the anger drained from his face, only to be replaced with complete impatience.

"What are you talking about?" Dylan asked. "You haven't said anything to me about this."

Shelby touched her husband's arm, giving him a reassuring squeeze. It was such a simple, natural action that it was amazing it had such a profound effect on Kendall. She couldn't imagine ever being so at ease with Jonas that a simple touch could bring out his volatile personality.

"There wasn't time," Shelby said. "But for the life of me, I can't see how she could know what she knows if something isn't amiss."

"We aren't talking 'amiss,'" Rose said. "I can't believe you would be so gullible as to be taken in by her vivid imagination."

"Fine," Kendall announced, standing in such a rush that her chair clattered to the floor. "Then let's just be honest here. I'll let Jonas explain to you what will happen on December 11. If I'm wrong, you are all welcome to continue thinking I'm some crazed soul. If I'm right, I would hope you would all have the decency to apologize for not believing the truth." Kendall took two steps toward the door; then, feeling spiteful, she turned to Rose and said, "If I have such a vivid imagination, why is it that you've told the whole town that your husband is away on business?"

Kendall marched up the stairs, her footsteps echoing through the silent house. "Dramatic exit," she mumbled with a sigh as she entered the yellow bedroom and closed and locked the door. "Dramatic and mean," she said, knowing full well she shouldn't have been so unkind to her aunt. "But she's not my aunt," she reminded herself as she fell onto the bed. "She just looks like her, talks like her—and doesn't know me from a houseplant."

She stood in the room, torn between the desire to throw something and the desire to burst into frustrated tears.

"Okay," she began, taking in a deep breath. "There has to be an explanation for all this. I just have to look at it objectively, as though I'm diagnosing a patient, only I'm the patient," she finished with a sad groan.

"I know my father didn't die at age five, but this Rose's brother did. Therefore..." She stopped to take a breath. "They are not the same person. They can be from the same family," she continued. "Like this Rose is some sort of distant relative of mine, which would explain why she looks the same. But what about Shelby?" she asked herself.

The question moved her to sit on the edge of the neatly made bed. "Well, this Shelby is married to a man named Dylan, which I'm sure is simply coincidence. And having an employee named Susan isn't all that weird. Susan is a popular name. The fact that she was raised in an orphanage instead of by her mother proves that she isn't the same as my Shelby, so that sorta explains her."

Yeah, right! her brain screamed. Lying back, she stared at the ornate plaster design on the ceiling and said, "Or maybe I've traveled to a place I simply can't explain and sure as hell don't understand."

JONAS SEEMED to have accepted the fact that Kendall preferred her old room to sharing one with him. His quiet acceptance didn't do much to improve her temperament.

In the ten days since her little tirade at dinner, no one except Mrs. McCafferty had even gone near her. Kendall wasn't about to apologize, though, not when she had nothing to apologize for. She was from another time and she needed help in order to get back. If Jonas and the others couldn't handle that, she didn't need their company.

"He's gone out," Mrs. McCafferty said as she entered the room.

Kendall nodded. "Thanks, I'll come down for breakfast now."

"This isn't right, Lady Revell. Newlyweds shouldn't be behaving the way you and His Lordship have been. It isn't natural."

"Tell him that," she countered as she violently brushed her hair back from her face. "He started it."

"But he's a proud man."

"Pride isn't gender specific," Kendall answered as she left the room. "Besides, he'll come around by day after tomorrow."

"What?" Mrs. McCafferty said as she followed Kendall down the steps.

"He'll have no choice but to rethink his position after he sees I was telling the truth. Then, perhaps he and I can negotiate some sort of peaceful coexistence."

"Peace isn't what he'll be wanting," Mrs. McCafferty mumbled.

"What are you talking about?" Kendall asked as she took the seat where Jeffreys held her chair. The ritual had started the day following the dinner disaster. As soon as Jonas left to do whatever it was he did every morning, Kendall ate her breakfast, walked in the garden, then returned to her room and refused even to set eyes on her husband.

"He hasn't been the same since you stopped speaking to him," she said, her face a mesh of worry. "I've never seen him so out of sorts before. I know for a fact he's gone to your door twice, but something keeps him from knocking and getting this settled."

"Arrogance," Kendall supplied before slipping a slice of melon into her mouth. "But his superior self is going to be taken down a peg or two before all this is over."

"It seems to me His Lordship isn't the only one around here with ego troubles," Mrs. McCafferty grumbled before she stomped from the room.

Great, Kendall thought. *Now my only friend is mad at me. Okay, so I do owe Rose an apology, but that's as far as I'm willing to bend.*

Kendall finished her breakfast without much enthusiasm. Slipping her cape on, she left by the back door, feeling renewed by the strong rays of the sun. One thing hadn't changed since her bizarre trip in time: she still needed the sun's rays to feel alive. The small building at the rear of the property housed the kitchen and was where Jeffreys and the two other housemen lived. Kendall knew she wasn't welcome there. Not because the three men disliked her, but because entertaining an unescorted white woman could cost them their lives. She contented herself by strolling along the pathway adjacent to the garden, trying to imagine what it would look like in the spring. "Not that I want to be here in the spring," she said aloud.

"You and Revell are planning on leaving Charleston?"

Kendall nearly jumped at the sound of Whitefield's voice. Turning in the direction of the offensive sound, she found him standing in the shadows of the dependency, dressed in full military regalia. In spite of the fact that her marriage to Jonas had all but guaranteed that this man couldn't arrest her, she felt a decent amount of unease knot her stomach.

"No," she answered in a clipped syllable. "What are you doing here?"

Whitefield smiled, but the gesture didn't reach his eyes. They were as cold as the wind coming off the water. "I see you're as forthright as I have been led to believe." It wasn't a compliment.

"I asked what you were doing here, Captain Whitefield. If you wish to speak to Jonas, I'm afraid—"

"No, ma'am," he interrupted with a polite inclination of his head.

He was so attractive that his actions could easily be construed as charming. But his charm was lost on Kendall. She was more interested in his motivations than his perfectly coiffed blond hair.

"I came specifically to speak with you."

"About what?"

His brows drew together as his hand rested on the handle of the sword tied at his hip. "Perhaps we would be more comfortable inside?"

"I doubt it," she answered honestly.

"I would appreciate some refreshment, Lady Revell, surely that isn't too much to ask, given the fact that your husband is so keen on adhering to social traditions."

"Fine," Kendall said with a sigh. "Follow me."

"With pleasure."

She recognized the double entendre and chose to ignore it. Whitefield trailed her inside, moving into the parlor as if he owned the place. He handed Jeffreys his hat and sword, then settled comfortably into one of the chairs.

"Is everything all right?" Mrs. McCafferty asked when she hustled into the room.

"The captain wanted a drink," Kendall explained. "Coffee, tea? What?"

"Tea would be lovely," he told Mrs. McCafferty in a superior tone that was dismissive and grating. "You're looking well," he said to Kendall as soon as they were alone.

"Is there some reason I shouldn't?" she challenged.

Whitefield's eyes filled with unabashed hatred. "Given the fate of Revell's last wife, it isn't totally unreasonable that some of us would have concerns for your safety."

"Unfounded and baseless concerns," Kendall said as she remained standing and crossed her arms in front of her. "If you simply wanted to assure yourself that I was still breathing, why waste Mrs. McCafferty's time by having her make tea?"

"You really are blunt, aren't you?"

Whitefield's facade was slipping. His cultured speech now held an edge that matched the harsh emotion in his piercing blue eyes.

"Among other things," she told him. "I'm also notoriously short on patience, so please get to the point."

"Very well," Whitefield said with a shrug. He waited for Mrs. McCafferty to place the tray on the table next to his chair and make her exit before he spoke. "The Grisom family has taken your—situation—rather hard."

"I'm sure," Kendall acknowledged.

"Revell's insensitivity is particularly disturbing in terms of his refusal to return certain rights to Mr. Grisom."

"If you're talking about the fact that Jonas received a fifty-percent share of the wharf for marrying Cecelia, I don't understand why you're discussing this with me."

"It was my hope that you could convince your husband to return those rights to Grisom, given the fact that Jonas killed—"

"You may leave now, Captain," Kendall cried. "And you will never be welcome here so long as you voice your baseless accusations regarding Cecelia's death."

Whitefield rose slowly and took a menacing step, which brought him right to Kendall. His hands reached out and grabbed her upper arms, painfully bruising the skin beneath the fabric.

"You really should be careful how you speak to me, Mrs. Revell. I hold an important position with the regiment currently in control of this area. If you don't—"

"If you don't get your hands off her, I'll kill you."

Whitefield's expression registered a healthy dose of alarm at Jonas's steely threat. After dropping his arms, he stepped away from Kendall and turned toward Jonas.

"I'm afraid you misunderstood."

"No, you didn't," Kendall said, meeting Jonas's questioning eyes. "He came here because he thought he could use me to get to you."

"Mrs. Revell?" Whitefield sputtered.

"That's *Lady* Revell," Jonas corrected. "Jeffreys!" The houseman appeared in a flash, Whitefield's hat and sword in his hands. "See the captain out."

"We need to get this settled, Revell," Whitefield argued.

"There is nothing to settle," Jonas responded. "You touch my wife again you're a dead man. Nothing ambiguous about that, now is there?"

"I wasn't talking about her. Grisom's wharf—"

"Is partially owned by me," Jonas finished. "Now, get out."

As soon as the door slammed, Jonas came over to Kendall, but stopped short of making physical contact. "Did he hurt you?"

"I'll probably have a few bruises, but nothing major."

Jonas let out a colorful expletive.

"I thought we weren't supposed to use that word," she teased.

His answer was a warm smile. It wasn't until that moment that Kendall realized just how much she had missed him.

"*You* aren't supposed to use that word," he explained. "Being a man does have its advantages."

Kendall needed no reminders of his masculinity. Not when he was standing close enough for her to catch the earthy scent that seemed to cling to his elegant riding habit. Not when she longed to reach up and brush the wayward strand of ebony hair from his face. Or trace the taut line of his jaw.

"I'm sorry if Whitefield upset you," he said in a voice that had gone suddenly soft and a half octave deeper. "I should have anticipated—"

Jonas never finished the sentence. He simply tossed his hat off into a corner and drew Kendall into his arms, kissing her almost painfully. Her back arched to accommodate his height, and she slipped her arms around his neck. The effects of the kiss instantly turned her bones to jelly.

Pride didn't seem to matter when he was holding her. In fact, nothing could even compare with the feelings she experienced whenever Jonas touched her. It was so overwhelming, so powerful, that it was almost frightening.

"I've missed you," he admitted several long minutes later when he reluctantly lifted his mouth from hers. His thumb came up to touch her slightly swollen lower lip. "I didn't mean to do that."

"I did," she told him. "Maybe we should try having a relationship where we only communicate with our bodies. We seem to get into trouble whenever we have a discussion."

"No talking, just touching?" he asked with a rakish grin. "I think you may be onto something."

While Kendall found his smile infectious, she wasn't quite willing to go that far to repair their strained relationship. "I could never do it," she told him. "I'm about as good at keeping my mouth shut as I am at obeying."

"I got that impression when you were so belligerent to Whitefield."

"You were eavesdropping?"

"Only for a second. Until that bastard grabbed you."

"Why is he over here threatening you on Grisom's behalf?"

"Good question," Jonas acknowledged. "Maybe because I already told Grisom I wasn't going to sign over my interest on the wharf."

"So he called in the troops?" she asked.

Jonas looked troubled. "Maybe." His arms came around and encircled her waist. "I've got to go out."

"But I thought—"

"Hush," Jonas soothed, placing a kiss on her forehead. "I'm having the same thoughts, too, which will make riding several miles on horseback damned difficult."

"Your language is surprising, Revell. Wherever did you learn to curse like a sailor?"

"My beautiful wife," he said as he gave her a brief kiss. "I'll be back by supper."

"Do we have to eat?" she teased, reaching behind him to give his derriere a squeeze.

"You'll need your strength, Kendall. Do tell Mrs. McCafferty to plan something quick. No six-course meals this night."

"Where are you going?" she asked, horrified to hear a whiny quality to her voice. She sounded amazingly like a nagging wife. "I mean," she corrected, "Do you have to go out?"

Jonas ran his finger in a tantalizing path along her jawline, sending shivers of anticipation through her. His eyes held a promise that thrilled her beyond imagination.

"I'm afraid I must go," he said softly.

"Must or should?"

Jonas glanced around, then placed his mouth very near her ear. Near enough so that she could feel the heat of his breath as it whipped through her hair.

"I have a meeting, Kendall. The information is essential if I'm to prevent bloodshed."

"What about your blood?" she persisted. "What if something happens to you?"

His smile was little reassurance.

"Worried for my safety?" he asked.

The smile turned rather smug and there was definite pleasure in the speculation.

"I'm a doctor, Jonas. I think people should live, not die."

The look he offered told her he didn't believe her noncommittal response.

"Don't concern yourself," he said easily. "I'll be back in time to spend the entire evening *entertaining* you."

Reluctantly, Kendall let him go after impulsively going up on her tiptoes to place a kiss in the general vicinity of his mouth.

"Be careful," she whispered several minutes later as she watched him mount and ride away from the window.

MRS. MCCAFFERTY'S MOOD improved dramatically when she learned that Kendall and Jonas would be dining together. Perhaps she was simply reacting to the way Kendall had blushed when she had asked the woman to prepare something fast and light.

Kendall busied herself with a bath and the arduous task of drying her long hair. "This is a royal pain," she grumbled as she shook her head near the roaring fire.

"What?" Mrs. McCafferty asked.

"No hair dryers, no electric rollers. None of the things that make life simple."

The older woman snorted and rested her hands on her ample hips. "And what else have you to do that you can't take the time to dry your hair."

"Good point," Kendall acknowledged. "I guess I just miss all the creature comforts I took for granted."

"I think it's His Lordship you're missing," she said without even trying to disguise her approval.

"Jonas does grow on you," Kendall conceded reluctantly. "Since I'm stuck with him, I might as well make the best of it."

"Stuck, my foot. You're developing a fondness for him. I can tell."

Kendall spared the woman a look. "Physical chemistry isn't fondness."

Mrs. McCafferty blushed. "I don't know about chemistry, but I do know about being suited. You and His Lordship are well suited. Not like that one my Colleen married. God forgive me, but I hope he's taken in the war so that she can have a second chance."

"Is he that bad?" Kendall asked.

"He's a mean one," she answered. "Takes his anger out on my Colleen when the mood strikes. She always has a handy excuse, but I don't hold to a man raising his fist in anger to his woman."

"I'll talk to her," Kendall said.

"Won't do no good. Colleen is about as dumb as a cow when it comes to that boy."

"But she has her son to think about," Kendall argued. "Get my gown. We'll go now. I have to remove her sutures anyway."

"But your hair—"

"Will dry eventually," Kendall finished.

They found Colleen in her modest home, lying in her small bed, feeding her beautiful infant son. Her green eyes showed signs of fatigue, but she seemed too enthralled with her new baby to mind the apparent lack of sleep.

"I came to remove your stitches," Kendall said as she took the baby, admired him for a minute, then handed him off to his proud grandmother.

Colleen shyly allowed Kendall to examine her for signs of infection as well as a few other potential problems. She cried out when Kendall removed the stitches with the crude scissors and tweezers she had brought along. Her face turned crimson when Kendall asked if she was having any trouble breast-feeding.

"No," the girl said, shielding her eyes as she unwillingly participated in the frank conversation.

"Colleen," Kendall began as she sat on the edge of the bed. "You and your son are alive because of major surgery, do you understand that?"

The girl nodded.

"You have to be extremely careful about your activities for the next several weeks. I'll make arrangements with Jonas to keep sending someone to help you each day. Your mother can—"

"No, please!" Colleen whispered. "I love her dearly, but my mother and I can't take a breath without fighting over it."

Kendall smiled. "Okay. But with the stitches out, you'll have to be very careful not to strain anything, do you understand?"

"Yes, ma'am."

"And no sexual intercourse."

"Lady Revell!" Colleen gasped. "My husband isn't even here."

"Well," Kendall said in her firmest "doctor" tone, "if he should happen to come home for a visit, he isn't to touch you in *any* way."

"James is really a good man at heart," she said.

"I'm sure he has some wonderful qualities," Kendall agreed. "But you have a son to care for now. If you raise that child in an environment where he sees his father beating you, he'll beat his wife. Just as bad, think about what you'll do when your husband beats him."

"James so wanted a son. He would never—"

"It isn't about love and wanting, Colleen. When a man hits a woman or a child, it's about power and domination. It also tends to run in families. So, if you don't want your son to grow up being abused or learning to abuse, get out."

"Was all that true?" Mrs. McCafferty asked as they walked slowly back to the Rose Tattoo in the dark.

"Unfortunately, yes."

"Your time must surely be better than this," she mused. "It sounds like women have a much better lot in life."

"Some things are better and others are worse," Kendall explained. Stopping, she placed her hand on the woman's arm and met her eyes. "Thank you for believing me."

"It goes against everything in nature," Mrs. McCafferty answered nervously. "But it is the only explanation for the likes of you."

Locking her arm with the older woman, Kendall picked up the pace. "Was that supposed to be a compliment? It sounded a little bit like 'Gee, that dress doesn't make you look quite so fat' to me."

"My apologies."

"It was a joke," Kendall assured her. When they turned the corner at East Bay, her heart fluttered when she saw the silhouette of a horse tethered at the railing. "I didn't expect him so soon," she said, forcing herself not to run, not to appear overanxious. *To hell with it,* she thought as she dropped Mrs. McCafferty's arm and lifted her skirts.

"You're not fond of him," Mrs. McCafferty called.

"No, ma'am."

Kendall ignored the woman's hoot of laughter, as she raced up the steps. Jeffreys opened the door, his face masked with concern. "What?" she asked.

"I didn't know where to find you. It's bad."

"Where is he?" she asked.

"We took him to his bed, ma'am."

Kendall rushed past the man and up the stairs. Jonas was on top of the bed, perfectly still, bleeding profusely.

Chapter Eleven

Kendall barked out orders, which unlike the first time, were followed without hesitation. Shelby, Rose and Dylan soon returned with the supplies.

"What can I do to help?" Dylan asked.

"Find whoever did this to him," Kendall answered as she poured alcohol over her hands.

"How bad is it?" Rose asked.

"The knife hit a major artery in the leg. He's lost a great deal of blood."

"What does that mean?" Shelby inquired.

"It means we don't have a lot of time," she replied before going to work.

Dylan proved to be a far better assistant than Jeffreys, and in no time, she had repaired the wound. But that wasn't her major concern. Jonas's pressure was dangerously low. Which made her wonder if he hadn't lost too much of his blood volume before she'd gotten to him.

"I can't risk transfusion. I have no way of determining his blood type in time, even if I did have the right equipment," she thought aloud.

"Transfusion?" Dylan asked.

Kendall explained the procedure. She was pretty sure she could rig a needle and some of the glass tubing to make it work; she just wasn't sure if she should do something so drastic.

"What are his chances?" Dylan asked.

Kendall felt Jonas's wrist. His pulse was too faint to be detected, so she moved her fingers to his throat. "He's lost too much blood," she admitted.

"Then let's do it."

"But if you and Jonas don't match, your blood might kill him."

Dylan was hastily shrugging out of his jacket and shirt. "It doesn't sound like we have a choice, ma'am. At least if we do this, we've tried."

"Tried what?" Shelby asked as she entered the room and moved toward the bed, obviously surprised to see her husband disrobing. Her expression paled when they explained what they were going to do. Dylan lay down carefully on the bed next to Jonas, while Mrs. Mc-Cafferty began a litany of prayers, and Rose set about creating what Kendall described with blown-glass tubing from one of the light fixtures, a wooden candle form and two syringes.

"This might sting," she warned Dylan as she swabbed the crease of his arm with brandy. Shelby was at his side, holding his hand. Making sure he remained upon the mound of pillows, since they had only gravity to make the procedure a success.

"It stings," Dylan said when she pierced his skin.

"Sorry," she mumbled. "Stay still. Rose, I need more light so I can try to judge the volume."

"Right here," the woman said, producing another candelabra as she stood at Kendall's side. "I sure hope you know what you're doing."

Ignoring Rose, Kendall kept two fingers on Jonas's artery and her eyes glued to the hastily flowing blood in the device. When she was satisfied that she had replaced enough of the vital fluid, she made quick work of disassembling everything.

"Hold that against your arm tightly and don't try to sit up yet," she told Dylan. Then, turning to look at Jonas, she said to Jeffreys. "Bend his arm up and keep pressure where I had the needle."

Kendall checked Jonas's pupils. Relief filled her when she saw no sign of major complication. "I think it worked," she said with a smile. "His pulse is stronger and he seems to be tolerating the transfusion."

"Stay there," she warned Dylan, who ignored her and very nearly fell face first on the floor. "Get him some fruit juice and something sweet. It will get rid of that woozy feeling."

"I can handle that," Mrs. McCafferty announced proudly.

"IS HE ANY BETTER?" Shelby asked when she joined Kendall in the parlor.

Seeing the two small children had a strange effect on Kendall. Chad and Cassidy eyed her warily. Chad normally ran to her, begging for a hug, while his younger sister was usually fascinated and content to play with

Kendall's fair hair. Now they cowered shyly at their mother's skirts. The rejection, though unintentional, was the last thing she needed in her current state. Ever since Jonas had spiked a high fever, Kendall had been on the verge of tears. She had no way of knowing whether his worsened condition was her fault. Was it a direct result of trying to do something with inadequate tools and untried methods?

"He's still feverish."

Shelby sat her children near the fire, giving them each a stick of what smelled like peppermint. "I'm sure he'll come around. Dylan hasn't suffered any ill effects from the treatment."

"He shouldn't have," Kendall answered almost numbly. "Rose came by this morning. She isn't speaking to me."

"She's taken Joe Don's abandonment quite hard," Shelby said.

"What could he possibly want here?"

"Who?" Shelby inquired as she came over and stood next to Kendall at the window. "Oh."

"I'm not in any mood to deal with yet another of Grisom's errand boys," Kendall announced just as Franklin Monroe knocked at the door. "Especially not that one."

Jeffreys announced the man just as he stepped into the room. Holding his hat and a gold-knobbed walking stick, the man looked like a lawyer. His clothing was conservative, as were the cut and style of his dark hair. His eyes were equally dark and set close together above a narrow, pointed nose.

"Lady Revell, Mrs. Tanner," he acknowledged politely.

"Jonas isn't dead yet," Kendall began without preamble. "So you've probably wasted a trip."

Monroe looked puzzled. "I'm afraid there must be some sort of misunderstanding."

"What does bring you here, Mr. Monroe?" Shelby asked as she pulled on the cord to summon Mrs. McCafferty. "Please be kind enough to take the children to another part of the house," she instructed when Mrs. McCafferty appeared.

Chad and Cassidy readily went with the woman, while Kendall kept her eyes on Monroe, trying to determine if his professed confusion was genuine.

"Your husband sent me," Monroe said to Shelby. "Mr. Tanner felt it was appropriate that I be the one to explain my position to Lady Revell."

"Your position on what?" Kendall asked.

"Your husband's... injury."

There was something about the way Monroe said the word that grated on her already overstressed nerves. "My husband was stabbed," Kendall corrected. "You make it sound like he hit his thumb with a hammer."

Monroe sucked in a breath and squared his shoulders. "You must understand the situation, Lady Revell. Wasting time and energy investigating what was, in all likelihood, a self-inflicted wound for the purposes of—"

"Back up!" Kendall cut in. "What makes you think Jonas's wound was self-inflicted. That has to be the dumbest thing I have ever heard? Especially since you haven't even seen the wound."

"Sheriff Tanner said you wouldn't be reasonable about this possibility."

"Reasonable?" Kendall challenged loudly. Ignoring the angry red stain seeping up from the man's neck, she continued, "I can assure you that Jonas did not stab himself."

"I'm sure it comforts you to believe that," Monroe said.

That patronizing, superior tone sent Kendall over the edge.

"Look, you spiteful little weasel. I think the only reason you have classified Jonas's stabbing as self-inflicted is that Caroline Grisom is your housemate. If you won't allow Dylan to investigate this crime so that someone can be prosecuted, you are obviously incapable of properly doing your job."

"Caroline is not the reason I believe Revell did this to himself."

"You have about two seconds to explain," Kendall warned.

The man glared down at her for a second. "You are either the most gullible woman around, or you have knowingly and willingly chosen to marry a murderer."

"Jonas hasn't murdered anyone," she insisted.

"Gullible," he snorted. "The man has obviously convinced you that he isn't responsible for throwing the loveliest creature in all of Charleston from the second story of this house."

"Hold it," Kendall instructed, raising her hand while she mentally weighed each and every word. Lifting her blue eyes in challenge, she said, "You loved her."

"Kendall," Shelby said in a whisper. "I don't think—"

"Of course I was in love with her," Monroe cried. "Most men were. To know Cecelia was to love her. With the one notable exception of Revell."

"If you were so in love with her and Grisom was in such an all-fire hurry to find her a husband, why didn't you marry her?"

Monroe didn't answer Kendall's question immediately. He seemed content to study the pattern of the wool rug.

"Well?" Shelby prompted. "I think you owe Lady Revell a response after all the accusations you have made regarding her husband. Who, by the way, is upstairs in quite poor condition."

That piece of information seemed to bring Monroe some amount of sick comfort. "I was never able to tell Cecelia of my feelings," he answered quietly. "And then he killed her."

"Jonas didn't kill anyone," Kendall repeated, reaching the end of her patience. "And since you don't have any intention of finding out who tried to kill him—for the second time, I might add—I would appreciate it if you would get the hell out of my house."

Kendall brushed the man's shoulder as she exited the room. As she saw it, her only options were either to leave, or to grab one of the irons from the fireplace and beat some sense into him.

"Lord, doesn't anyone in this time think logically?" she grumbled as she reached for the knob and entered Jonas's darkened bedroom.

"I've been rubbing him with alcohol every hour, just as you said," Jeffreys said.

"Is there any change?"

"He's still burning up."

"I'll sit with him for a while," Kendall told him after she gave his small shoulder a reassuring squeeze. "Go get something to eat, and please tell Mrs. McCafferty I won't be needing her to make dinner for me."

"You haven't eaten all day, ma'am."

"I'll grab something later," she mumbled as she climbed up on the high bed and felt the heat emanating from Jonas's sweaty body. She checked his pupils and his pulse, feeling utterly and totally helpless. His wound was clean, but that didn't mean she hadn't missed something when she'd sutured.

"Please don't die, Jonas," she whispered as she took a cloth and dabbed away the moisture.

He groaned and his head moved in the direction of her voice.

"You have to fight this infection and get well," she told him. "I'm afraid, for the first time in my life. I'm afraid to live in this world without you. You do get on my nerves at times, because you can be pretty sexist, but I really don't think I could stand it if you died."

"Kendall?" he rasped, though his eyes didn't open.

"I'm here," she said. "What happened, Jonas? Who did this?"

"Kendall . . . love you."

"Jonas, you don't know what you're saying, but at least you're talking. Tell me what happened so I can tell Dylan."

"Has to be love . . . need you too much."

"Hush," she said as she filled a glass with water and brought it to his lips. "Try to drink, Jonas. You need fluids."

"Need . . . you . . . to . . . stay."

"I'm not going anywhere," she told him. "Please try to take a sip."

In his current state, there was no way he could identify his attacker. She held his head and managed to get a few ounces of water into him before he faded out again. His color looked better, she decided about half an hour later when she realized he was no longer perspiring and his skin felt cooler to the touch. He was still pale, but his vital signs were encouraging.

She was so excited she was just about to ring for Mrs. McCafferty, when the door burst open and a very breathless Rose appeared.

"My God, Kendall, you were right. Just about the whole city is on fire."

All through the night of December 11, what few men were left inside the city stood with the Confederate soldiers and managed to battle the flames as building after building ignited. When it was all over, the fire had destroyed everything from the sail and blind factory at the foot of Hasell Street to the east end of Tradd, basically claiming an area of 540 acres between the Ashley and Cooper rivers.

"SHE WAS RIGHT, you know," Rose told Jonas as she sat in a chair next to his bed. "It was just as she said it would be."

"I know."

"What do you think it means?"

Jonas studied his friend, knowing she was as skeptical as he, yet the evidence seemed to support the strange claims of his beautiful bride. "I have no idea," he said as he stretched his frame, tired from the week of lying in bed.

"Is it possible that she really did travel through time? That she isn't real?"

"She's real," Jonas said without hesitation. "I suppose anything is possible," he amended, hoping to sound philosophical. "She could prove to be invaluable to us."

Rose's look was disapproving. "If what she has been saying is true, then she is part of my family. I won't have you using her if it means putting her in danger."

"But she must know a great deal about the major turning points in the war. If she can tell me of those with the same accuracy she predicted the fire—"

"Maybe that's all it was," Rose suggested. "Just a lucky prediction. Or maybe she overheard something."

Jonas shook his head. "Her knowledge of medicine isn't luck. She has saved my life on two occasions."

One of Rose's brows arched high on her forehead. "Have you ever stopped to wonder why?"

"Because she's a doctor."

Rose nodded. "That must be why she barely left your side in all the time you were ill. It wasn't until you started mumbling that she went off to try to help some of the victims burned or injured by the fire."

"Did my stores make it?"

Rose shook her head. "Most of the cotton stores were lost. But I didn't come here to discuss cotton."

"I'm sorry," Kendall said, as she peeked around the corner of the partially opened door.

Jonas immediately noticed the fatigue around her eyes, as well as the soot, ash and filth that were smudged on her cheeks.

"Come in," he said, struggling to keep his voice even. Regardless of her current state of disarray, he didn't want her to leave.

She seemed nervous as she joined them, and he noted that she never made eye contact.

"You surely are a sight," Rose said. "And when was the last time you slept?"

"That's why I came back," Kendall answered. "I'm about dead on my feet."

"What exactly have you been doing?" Jonas queried.

"A small hospital was set up. I've been helping Dr. Faraday and Miss Whitefield tend to people."

"Helping?" Jonas asked.

Her smile was almost one of embarrassment. "Okay, so I felt it was my duty to teach that quack the right way to salve and wrap a serious burn."

"Lily Whitefield must have loved that," Rose commented. "She thinks Faraday walks on water, and I'll bet she didn't take too kindly to your making him look like a jackass in front of others.''

Kendall wiped her palms on the front of her skirt. He noted that there were several other smeared stains, indicating that she had been working a long time.

"She tried to have me tossed out on more than one occasion," Kendall answered. "But I guess, in the end, people were in such pain they didn't care who treated them."

"Rose?" he asked as he shifted himself to a sitting position. "Would you mind giving Kendall and me a moment?"

Rose was out of the chair instantly. After kissing the air in the vicinity of his cheek, she moved to Kendall. The two women stood toe-to-toe and Jonas held his breath, not knowing what his longtime friend intended.

"I never thought I'd have a niece," she said with just a hint of emotion in her voice. "Welcome to the family."

"Do you mean it?" Kendall asked, her blue eyes shrouded with caution.

"I think so," Rose answered. "I can't seem to come up with a better explanation for all your talents."

"What about you?" she asked as soon as Rose had left. "Do you believe me?"

His eyes met hers and he searched her expectant face for a long time. "I have to admit that from the stories I've been hearing, I don't really have much choice."

He hadn't expected her to fling herself onto the bed, but she did. Jonas didn't mind; in fact, he wished she might have done this days ago. The feel of her small body was a sensation burned into his mind, and he had thought of her almost every waking moment. *What has happened to me?* he wondered. How could she have become this important to him in such a short period of time? And how would he bear it if, and when, she found a way to return to her own time? How could he feel the way he felt and stand in her way? God, either possibility brought with it a profound sense of sadness and loss. So profound that he felt the need to communicate his fears to her, perhaps convince her to stay with him.

Taking her smudged face in his hands, he kissed her gently, silently hoping things would never have to change.

"What was that all about?" she asked, when he set her away from him and brushed some of the hair off her face.

"I believe it was a kiss," he said, trying to add lightness to his heavy heart. "You have indicated in the past that you enjoy being kissed."

Her eyes narrowed as she listened. "You're lying, Jonas. That was something different. You look like you just lost your best friend. Has something happened?"

He shrugged and tried to force a smile to his lips. "I lost a great deal in the fire," he hedged. "But I suppose that is nothing compared with the poor souls who lost more than just material possessions."

She nodded, then yawned. "I'll change your dressing, then I really need a quick bath and a nap before I go back."

"Go back?" Jonas asked. "Surely the worst is over now."

"It is, but that doesn't mean I can't do some good."

"You can do some good here," he said with a playful wink.

She shook her head and placed her hands on her slender hips. "You're incorrigible, Jonas Revell. I can't believe you're the same man who was mumbling deliriously just a short time ago."

"What makes you think I was delirious?"

"I heard what you said," she told him with a nervous giggle. "Believe me, you'd be as red as a beet if I repeated even half of it."

"I think I said—"

"It isn't important," Kendall cut in on a rush of breath. "I didn't take any of it seriously, and I know it was the fever talking and not you."

"But, Kendall—" he said, trying again.

"Really, Jonas. I've got to go now. I want you to stay in bed until at least tomorrow."

Frowning, he decided she wasn't in a terribly receptive mood. Funny that a woman who could curse like a man, discuss sexuality as if it were the weather, wasn't, apparently, inclined to discuss matters of the heart. Specifically not her own heart.

"I guess we can talk about my...delirium another time."

"Fine," she said, visibly relieved. "I'm going to get cleaned up and grab a nap."

"You can sleep with me," he suggested, turning down a corner of the sheet.

She gave him a lopsided look. "I don't think that would work, nor would it be particularly good for your leg."

"You're a doctor. Surely you can figure out a way for us to—"

"I'm leaving now, Jonas," she interrupted, her face flaming. "You need to get your strength back."

"Why don't you give me a reason? You know, some sort of reward if I promise to be a good boy."

"I'll bet you were never a good boy," she answered with a laugh. "Besides, I can't think of a single thing I could offer as a reward," she said with a playful twinkle in her eyes.

"I have a few suggestions."

"All of them X-rated, no doubt."

"X-rated?"

"Sexually explicit," she corrected. "Obviously, your libido wasn't hurt."

"Want to test your theory, Doctor?"

Her expression grew suddenly serious. "I'm glad you believe me, Jonas. It means a lot to me."

He suddenly realized he didn't want gratitude from Kendall. He wanted much more. Recalling her belief that she would return to her time if she was able to prove he didn't kill Cecelia, Jonas stroked the stubble on his chin. "I'll think about your suggestion."

"Which suggestion?" she asked.

"That I permit you to examine Cecelia's body."

Her eyes grew wide. "Thank you."

"I haven't said yes," he cautioned. "Just that I would consider it."

"Why the sudden change of heart?"

"Because if you do manage to prove me innocent, you can return to your time."

"Right."

The hurt in her voice from that one word haunted him long after she had hastily left the room. Still, he didn't dare read more into it.

"NOT NOW, please," Kendall whispered when she saw Caroline coming toward her on the street. She was too exhausted from her hectic day to deal with the girl.

"Stop!"

"Go away, Caroline," Kendall warned. "I'm tired and—" She met the girl's eyes. "Jonas is waiting for me."

Caroline flinched, but she stood her ground, effectively preventing Kendall from passing. She thought of simply knocking the girl on her fanny into the dirty street, but that required an expense of energy, and Kendall preferred to save what little energy she had for later, now that Jonas was up and about.

"I know Franklin came to see you."

"Franklin, Whitefield, all your father's flunkies have dropped in."

"You have to get Jonas to listen to reason," Caroline insisted.

Maybe it was the slight catch in the girl's voice, or perhaps just the fact that she seemed suddenly scared.

"I don't have any interest in telling Jonas what to do with his interest in the wharf. As far as I'm concerned, it's between him and your father."

"But he should leave Charleston," Caroline persisted. "It's what he should have done after Cecelia died."

A sound of utter disbelief rumbled from Kendall's throat. "This is his home," she reminded the girl. "And Fairhaven, as well. Why on earth would he leave Charleston?"

"Because of Cecelia's death."

"Look," Kendall began, calling on her reserve of patience and constantly reminding herself that this girl had recently lost her sister. "Jonas didn't kill her, so there isn't any reason he should consider relocating."

"But he can go back to England," Caroline whined. "Captain Whitefield has always wanted to buy Fairhaven, and Father needs full control of the wharf."

"*Needs* or wants?" Kendall asked, growing tired of the pointless conversation.

"It is the only thing of value he has. He's desperate."

"I'm really very sorry," Kendall said as she lifted her skirts with the intention of stepping into the street to get past the annoying girl.

"But Jonas *has* to leave!" she cried.

"That's ridiculous. Now, if you'll excuse me—"

"I was there that night," Caroline said, lowering her voice to a near whisper. "I saw him do it. I saw Jonas kill Cecelia."

Chapter Twelve

"You seem nervous," Jonas observed, his eyes following her as she paced back and forth in front of the fireplace.

"I had an interesting chat with Caroline on my way home," she said. "You certainly have managed to make the Grisoms angry, haven't you?"

Shrugging his broad shoulders, Jonas leaned against the mantel, shifting some of the weight off his bad leg. "Grisom blames me for his daughter's death."

"No wonder," she said, meeting his eyes. "Caroline just told me that she saw you kill Cecelia."

"What?" he bellowed.

Kendall offered a reassuring smile. "Don't worry, she wasn't very convincing."

She watched as relief and apparent pleasure lightened his expression. Jonas seemed to approve of the fact that she hadn't given much credence to Caroline's dramatic proclamation.

"If she told Grisom that story, it's no wonder he's so bitter."

"She did shed some light on why I've had so many visitors, though."

"Which is?"

"Does Whitefield want Fairhaven?"

The smile that formed on his chiseled mouth could only be described as derogatory. "I bought the land for back taxes when I first came here. I rebuilt the house and returned it to its present condition. Whitefield has made no secret of his belief that I stole the place away from his family."

"Then why didn't he just pay the taxes?"

"At the time, Whitefield's family had suffered three straight years of failed crops."

"So you did the corporate-raider thing and now he's pissed."

Jonas was gaping at her.

"Sorry," she mumbled. "I know some of my expressions are foreign to you, but sometimes it is just as hard for me. The use of the word 'Madam' in my time usually refers to a woman who runs a brothel. I'll try to remember where I am while I'm stuck here, okay?"

She watched as his expression closed. It was like watching a heavy wall fall into place.

"What?"

He shook his head and moved over to refill his glass. He drank the glass of brandy in one quick swallow.

Troubled by the sudden change in him, Kendall went to his side, placing a tentative hand on his forearm. "What's wrong, Jonas?"

She heard his audible breath and felt the muscle beneath her fingers tense.

"I suppose I have grown rather accustomed to having you around these past weeks. Whenever you speak of leaving..."

"Jonas," she began softly, giving him a gentle tug so that his eyes met hers. "I can't figure out how to get back, but if I do you have to understand my side of it."

The words sounded shallow to Kendall, even as she allowed them to slip past her lips. Damn it! She wasn't supposed to feel this emptiness whenever she thought about going home. About leaving him behind.

"I'm trying, Kendall."

"I know what happens," she continued. "I know that this is the costliest war this country has yet to experience. I know that people of vision and greatness are assassinated."

"You could help prevent those things," he suggested.

Kendall nodded. "I've thought about that. But what if I were to somehow change the course of history? What if I said or did something that had a negative effect later on?"

"Such as?"

Pressing her fingers against her temples, Kendall searched her memory. "Let's say Lincoln gets reelected and serves a second term as president."

"Does that happen?"

Kendall nodded, averting her eyes in the process. "But in that second term, his plans could prevent this country from hearing the voices of Martin Luther King, Jr. And Maya Angelou."

"Who are they?"

"Just two examples of great visionaries, whose futures I could affect if I started fooling around with the past."

"But we can prevent bloodshed," Jonas argued, his large hands coming up to grip her upper arms. "With your help, I could prevent what you're telling me will be a long, awful period with a lot of needless death and suffering."

She looked at the deep lines etched at the corners of his eyes; the sincerity she saw there touched her deeply. "It wouldn't be right, Jonas. Who knows? I may have already done or said something that will change the course of things. That's why it is so important that I get back to where I belong."

His expression grew solemn. "I understand," he said quietly. "I suppose you'll need this." Jonas reached into the pocket of his trousers and removed the locket. Lifting her hand, he placed the locket in her palm, then wrapped her fingers around it. The locket held the warmth of his body. His eyes were anything but warm.

"Thank you," she said, barely able to get the words out over the lump in her throat. "I don't know what to say..."

His palm flattened against her cheeks and his eyes studied each of her features. Kendall's heart actually hurt when she realized he was trying to commit her to his memory.

"I wish there were some other way," he said. "I wish I could find a way to make you want to stay here."

"And I wish I knew a way to take you with me."

He smiled. "That would be perfect, wouldn't it? Is there war in your time?"

She nodded. "But not like this. We've made it very neat and sanitary. Enemies can kill each other without ever coming face-to-face."

"Hmm, that would make it simpler, I suppose."

Jonas reached his hands around her waist and pulled her against him. "Your leg..." she protested weakly.

"Is just fine," he promised.

"But we shouldn't be doing this, not so soon after your injury."

"Is that your medical opinion, or are you just trying to get out of your wifely duties?" he teased.

Placing her palms against his solid chest, Kendall allowed her fingernails to gently rake the outline of muscle. "I happen to enjoy my wifely duties very much. But we really shouldn't put undo stress on that leg."

Jonas kissed her forehead. "And what if I simply ignore your protests and carry you up to my bedroom and have my way with you?"

"We'd probably both break our necks, since your leg can barely hold your own weight, let alone mine."

He sighed, apparently resigned to following her advice in spite of his obvious desire. The hardness pressed against her belly left no doubt about that.

"So what should we do?" he asked.

"You can tell me what happened the night you were stabbed. God knows Monroe has all but forbidden Dylan to do any investigating."

Jonas shrugged. "Monroe just doesn't believe me."

"Because Monroe was madly in love with Cecelia. That's what he can't get over."

"Where did you hear this bit of gossip?"

"From him."

Placing a quick kiss on his lips, Kendall stared up at him, puzzled by his suddenly cheery mood. "I would think that hearing another man was in love with your wife would be a little depressing."

Jonas met and held her gaze. "It would be if he'd been talking about you."

"Be serious," she said, feeling her whole body go still at this sudden change in the direction of their conversation.

"I am," Jonas said, punctuating the remark with a slow, sensual kiss that actually left her breathless. "I know you don't want to discuss this, Kendall, but—"

"Hush," she said, placing her finger to his lips. "We don't have a future and this is hard enough without complicating it with our emotions."

"Are you really so able to turn your feelings on and off like that, Kendall?"

"I've had to learn to do that, Jonas. If not, I wouldn't be able to cope with my job. Emotional distance is a necessary defense mechanism for me."

"What about me?" he asked. "Am I just supposed to pretend that I don't—"

"Yes," she cut in. "We can make it wonderful for however long I'm here," she said, hoping to salve some of the pain she read in his expression. "Or, we can have pointless conversations that won't change a thing."

Reluctantly, he inclined his head fractionally.

"Good. Now, since we can't do what we'd like to be doing, why don't you explain to me why you're working with a slimeball like Maitland?"

Jonas reluctantly allowed her to slip from his embrace. Kendall took a seat close to the fire, while Jonas sank into the chair, then lifted his injured leg onto the ottoman. "Aren't you going to put it on?" he asked, nodding to the locket she still clutched in her hand.

"In a minute," she hedged. "I want to know more about you and Maitland."

"Maitland is a necessary evil."

"Evil enough to have stabbed you? Is that what happened?"

"I was on my way to meet a new contact, when a rider came out of the trees and attacked."

"Was it someone you know—like Maitland or Whitefield?"

Jonas shook his head. "It happened really quickly and my horse threw me. By the time I recovered, the man had disappeared back into the trees."

"But you did recognize him?" Kendall guessed.

"It was pitch-black, yet there was something familiar about him. But I really couldn't say who it was."

Kendall moved next to him, placing her hand on one of his. "Think, Jonas. Could you see his face, maybe his hair? A hand with a ring or something?"

"He was completely shrouded by a cape. I only got a look at his boots."

"That's a start."

He sighed. "Not really. I only caught a glimpse and all I can remember is that they were black and well-worn."

"I'll assume there's no such thing as Pay-Less Shoes yet, so couldn't we get a list of all the men in Charleston who have had black boots made?"

Jonas tapped the arm of the chair with his finger. "I'm quite certain it would take from now until your time for us to track down every man who has commissioned black riding boots."

"That many, huh?" she asked, deflated.

"And as I said, they were well-worn, so the person could very well have had them made a number of years ago, in any town or city with a cobbler."

"I get your point," Kendall said. "Investigation is much simpler in my time. We can trace dye lots to specific manufacturers, then trace the finished product through distributors. Computers make it pretty easy to gain access to all sorts of information."

"Computers?"

"Machines that store and manipulate all sorts of information. They control most everything, much to the chagrin of my lab tech, who would probably be much happier if we did everything by abacus and stone tablets."

"Your computer sounds much more interesting," Jonas said, intrigue obvious in his large eyes. "What other marvels do you have?"

"Television, movies and my personal favorite," she said with a smile, "the CD player." Kendall went on to explain these things in great detail. Jonas hung on her every word, stopping her occasionally to ask questions.

He let out a long whistle. "I think I would like your time."

"I think so, too," she said softly. "Why do you work with Maitland against the South?"

"My reasons are quite simple. I don't believe any good can come of civil war. History would testify to that. I really have only one goal in life and it is not terribly lofty."

"Which is?"

"To live in peace at Fairhaven. To continue to make improvements to the architecture and the grounds. I like creating things, designing things. I was happiest when Fairhaven was under construction."

"You'll get a chance to do it over again," Kendall commented.

His dark brows drew together at the bridge of his nose. "Fairhaven is destroyed?"

Kendall was sorry she had opened her mouth. "I honestly don't know," she told him. "I just know that by my time, it isn't standing. At least most of it isn't."

Jonas closed his eyes and leaned his dark head against the back of the chair. "I built that place in the hope that it would continue long after my death. That is the tradition in England, and I had wanted to continue it over here."

"Now that I've told you, maybe you can take measures to protect it. Unless it's your heirs who allow it to fall into ruin."

"What heirs?" he asked, without opening his eyes. "That will be unlikely once you leave here."

Kendall didn't know what to say. "I'm sure you'll find—"

"Another woman like you?" he finished with a sneer. "I know you don't want to hear this, Kendall, but I find I don't want any other woman but you."

"Jonas, don't," she pleaded.

Ignoring her protest, he reached out and pulled her into his lap. "I must be totally daft, but I know I've never felt like this before."

His mouth closed on hers, moving with exquisite tenderness. The fierce passion was tempered by something else, something that began to pierce the wall around Kendall's heart. Fireworks exploded in her mind as she slipped her arm around his neck and settled comfortably against him. She wished they could stay like this forever. Wished that lifetimes didn't stand between them.

Jonas lifted his head and reached out to grab her hand. He found the locket still clutched there and took it from her. "If you're going to leave me, Kendall, do it now, please?"

Lowering her head, she allowed him to slip the locket over her head. Nothing happened.

"It still doesn't work," she said, amazed by the fact that a part of her was glad. "I'm still doing something wrong."

Jonas rose, gently setting her on the floor. He didn't meet her eyes when he said, "You came to me on the grounds of Fairhaven. Perhaps when I take you there tomorrow morning, you'll have better...luck.''

"I thought Fairhaven was too dangerous," she reminded him.

"It is, but it is where Cecelia is buried."

"What are you saying?"

"Prove I didn't kill her, Kendall. The faster you accomplish that, the faster we can end this."

"YOU'RE ACTING like I *chose* this," she said, as she sat across from him in the carriage.

"You made a choice, Kendall." He kept his face turned toward the small window, refusing even to look at her. "I'm simply complying with your wishes."

Remembering the fireworks she experienced in his arms, Kendall reached out and took his hand. "Do you want to know what I really wish could happen?" she challenged, pinching his knee until she had his full attention. "I wish I could find whatever trapdoor I fell through and take you back with me. I've waited all my life to feel the things you make me feel. I had pretty much given up on that fairy tale until I met you. I don't know how it happened, but I'm in love with you, Jonas. The thought of leaving breaks my heart."

His jaw dropped open. "How can you tell me this now? Don't you know that I feel the same way about you?"

Tears welled up in her eyes. "Of course I know, but it doesn't change anything. It can't. I don't belong here and I never will."

He leaned forward and wiped a stray tear from her cheek. "You could, Kendall. We can leave the country until the war is over if you want. We could—"

"But what would that do to the course of things?" she countered, angry suddenly at fate and whatever else was responsible for her predicament. "You are a part of the war. If you suddenly disappear, it could change something that could affect dozens, maybe hundreds, of other things."

Jonas punched the seat next to him. "Then tell me what we're supposed to do. Am I just to forget you?"

"We have to. You'll just have to pretend that I died or something."

"Forgive me, but I wasn't heartbroken when Cecelia died. I was sorry for her passing, but it was never like this. Cecelia and I never shared what I've shared with you. Losing you might just be more than I can tolerate."

"Please don't say that," Kendall pleaded. "It isn't any easier for me, but we have no choice."

"Is that why you're wearing the locket?" he asked, accusation dripping from each syllable. "You want to make sure you're prepared at every step."

Kendall glared at him. "I'm wearing it because it has your picture inside."

"And that's all I'm to have of you, isn't it?" he asked quietly. "The photographs from the wedding."

The carriage stopped then, depositing them at the front of the stately mansion just as dusk turned the cool air a deep purplish blue.

Jonas and Kendall dined in total silence before he dismissed the staff and retrieved her satchel from the carriage.

"Thank you," she said, trying to keep her voice light. If her plan worked and she discovered something that could clear Jonas's name, she didn't want their last words spoken in anger.

His only response was a grunt.

So much for what I want, she thought as she followed him from the house. Apparently, he was going to make this as unpleasant as possible.

Jonas carried a candle as they followed a stone path that wound deep into the pines lining the property. After a short while, they came upon an iron gate that surrounded a crypt.

"Being kept aboveground will help," Kendall said.

"Spare me the details," Jonas told her in clipped tones. "I'll wait for you out here."

"Can I have a kiss?' she asked, standing in front of him.

Jonas looked over her head and said, "I have no desire to kiss you."

Taking a calming breath, Kendall swore she wouldn't cry as she entered the musty room and went to work. When she emerged more than two hours later, their roles had reversed.

"Your examination didn't send you back," Jonas observed happily, lifting her into his arms and attempting to kiss her.

"Put me down," she commanded as she twisted her head to keep from being subjected to his unwanted kiss.

"What happened? What did you discover?"

Kendall took the satchel and shoved it hard against his midsection. "I discovered you're a stinking liar."

"Kendall, I didn't kill her!"

"I'm not talking about that. Everything I found was consistent with a fall. There was only one unusual finding."

"What?"

"I'm referring to the fact that your wife—the one you didn't love and never touched—was three months pregnant when she died."

Chapter Thirteen

"We have to talk about this," Jonas insisted as he followed her into the bedroom.

"There's nothing to talk about," Kendall replied stiffly. "You've been lying to me from the word go. There's nothing you could say to me now that could—"

"Kendall!" Jonas thundered. "Think for a minute. What possible reason would I have for lying about my relationship with Cecelia? I would have looked much better in the eyes of all of Charleston had I professed undying love for my wife and unborn child." He moved to the window and pushed aside the curtain, allowing moonlight to spill into the dimly lit room. "Are you sure she was expecting?"

"Positive," Kendall answered, her anger fading somewhat as her rational side regained control over her emotions.

"I wasn't the father. But it does explain why Harris was in such an all-fire hurry to give me a portion of the wharf to marry Cecelia. He must have known about the baby."

"Then why come to you? Why wouldn't he just go to the father and demand that he do the honorable thing?"

"Maybe the father is already married," Jonas suggested. "Or maybe he did and the father said no."

"I'll bet if we find the father of Cecelia's child, we'll find out who is behind the attempts on your life."

"You're welcome to try," Jonas said "But I wouldn't even know where to begin."

"Harris Grisom probably won't be inclined to help us," Kendall stated. "Caroline, either. Franklin Monroe told me he loved her. It must be him."

"Franklin Monroe?" Jonas repeated. "The man's every action is dictated by his mother. I don't think he would have bedded Cecelia without his mother's permission."

"Jonas!" Kendall laughed. "That isn't kind."

"My apologies," he said with a deep bow. "But I find it hard to believe that I could have offended your sensibilities, dear wife. You aren't exactly easy to shock."

His expression darkened as his eyes made a bold appraisal of her. "Since we have been discussing my truthfulness, I feel it only appropriate that I tell you that I have lied to you in the past."

"Really?"

He closed the distance between them in a few long strides. "I lied when I refused to kiss you earlier. I can think of nothing that would give me more pleasure," he said, bending down.

He kissed her with a hard, hungry pressure that thrilled her. Her hands lifted quickly to his shirt, tearing open the edges in order to feel the rough silkiness of the dark hair covering his chest. She pushed the garment down his arms, feeling the power in his bunched muscles.

"I'm not sure I like your aggressive tendencies," he teased as he allowed what was left of his shirt to fall to the floor. "But I guess two can play your game."

That said, Jonas grasped the top of her bodice and tore the fabric to the waist. The noise she made against his mouth wasn't one of protest; it was sheer pleasure knowing that he wanted her as desperately as she wanted him. Dresses were replaceable. This sort of passion came along only once in a lifetime.

His mouth slowed to a gentler pace as his hand cupped the swell of her breast. Kendall moaned and pressed herself against him, caught between wanting this to last all night and the overwhelming urgency coiling her stomach.

She got both her wishes. Weeks of abstinence led to a quick, volatile joining. Then, slowly, while the rest of the house slept, they took their time exploring each other, whispering words of love as night gave way to dawn.

"We should try to get some sleep," Jonas suggested as she lay curled in the curve of his arm. "I have to be back in town by dinnertime."

"Don't tell me," Kendall groaned. "You've got another meeting. Another dangerous meeting?"

She felt and heard the laughter rumble deep in his chest.

"Nothing so cloak and dagger, I'm afraid. I simply have to be on time to receive a package."

"From Rose?"

She felt him tense for an instant.

"How did you know?"

"When you told me only three people knew you were a spy and you wouldn't reveal the third name, I realized it had to be Rose or Shelby."

"How did you decide on Rose?" Jonas took a lock of her hair and toyed with it as they spoke.

"I heard you talking."

Jonas let out a breath and gave her a gentle shake. "I warned you against eavesdropping."

"And I warned you that I don't obey very well."

Dropping the lock of her hair, Jonas reached down and slowly pulled the locket out from beneath the sheet. "I've grown to detest this thing."

"Think of it as a necessary evil, like Maitland."

"Right."

"Speaking of him," Kendall said as she propped herself up on her elbows. "I know why you spy for the Union. Why does he?"

"Money," Jonas answered. "He is making a small fortune, which he keeps secreted in banks in New York."

"And Rose? Why does she do it?"

"Even though it has been years since her husband left, Rose can't seem to get past it. Every month she pretends to receive a letter from him. The truth is, the last she heard, Joe Don Porter had his own regiment in Virginia. I think she's hoping he won't have the chance to return home to the young woman he left her for.''

Kendall shook her head. ''He did the same thing in my time,'' she told him. ''He left her and took their two young sons with him.''

Jonas was looking up at her with utter amazement in his eyes. ''Does she get her boys back?''

''You mean Joe Don took the boys this time, too?''

Jonas nodded.

''Eventually,'' Kendall answered. She didn't have the heart to tell him just how long and difficult that reunion would be.

''SO, WHAT DO YOU plan to do about it?'' Rose asked.

He shrugged, distracted with watching Kendall out in the garden with Chad and Cassidy. She seemed so natural with children that his mind took the normal route, and he wondered what it would be like for her to have his children.

''Jonas!'' Rose bellowed.

''Don't get cross,'' Shelby said, pouring them each a cup of tea in the process. ''This is all very difficult to digest.''

''Well, we can't breathe a word to anyone,'' Rose instructed. ''People wouldn't have the first notion what to do with a woman who wasn't real.''

''She is real,'' Jonas reminded her. ''And no one should know that better than I.''

Shelby blushed, but Rose seemed to derive smug pleasure from what his words implied. "Then you must think of a way to convince her to stay."

"I might not need to," Jonas answered, feeling that surge of guilt well up inside him. "She doesn't know how to get back to her time."

"That's wonderful!" Rose gushed. "That solves the problem of keeping her here."

"But it doesn't," Jonas admitted, feeling his shoulders slump forward. "I don't want her kept here as a prisoner. If she stays, I want it to be because it is what she wants. Or..." He decided that thought should remain unspoken.

"Or what?" Rose asked, her brow arched high and disapprovingly on her forehead.

"Perhaps there might be some way for me to accompany her back to her time."

"Jonas!" the women yelped in unison.

Shaking his head, he said, "It's probably a moot point anyway. Kendall has spent hours manipulating the locket. She tried taking my picture out, putting it in. She even repeated the words she had said just before it happened."

"She really is determined," Shelby said.

"Yes."

"Then you have to change her mind," Rose insisted. "It shouldn't matter where you are if you both love each other."

"But it does," Jonas said, repeating Kendall's argument. "She can't be a doctor, she doesn't have the same freedoms and she's terrified she'll do or say something that will change the course of world events.''

''Phooey,'' Rose said. ''I'll have a talk with the girl—make her see reason.''

That made Jonas smile. ''You're welcome to try.''

''WHERE'S JONAS?'' Kendall asked when she appeared for dinner and found Rose seated at the end of the table.

''He had to run an errand. He said if he wasn't back in time we should—''

''Is he in danger?'' Kendall asked, feeling her forehead crease from her frown. Rose's smile was sly, and it was all too reminiscent of the Aunt Rose whom Kendall knew so well. ''What is he doing?''

''He's out getting something for you, if you must know.''

Kendall felt the tension drain from her shoulders and she took her seat. ''Good. I'm kind of tired of stitching him back together after each of his clandestine adventures.''

''Jonas is a tough one,'' Rose said with genuine fondness. ''And now he has a good reason to come home in one piece.''

Eyeing her dinner companion cautiously, Kendall asked, ''What is that supposed to mean.''

''A man in love doesn't usually take so many risks.''

''Did he really have an errand, or did you send him off so that you and I could talk about this? Which—'' Kendall paused to make a production out of flipping her linen napkin into her lap "—*is none of your business.*"

Rose grunted. "Are you telling me you don't love him?"

"I'm telling you it is none of your business."

"I'm your aunt."

"Not for another hundred-plus years."

"I can't sit back and watch you destroy him. I've known Jonas for years and he's never been in love, to my knowledge."

"I don't want to hear this," Kendall said.

"Well, someone has to say it. I think I understand why you want to go back to wherever you came from, but you'd lose a good man in the process. Is it really worth it?"

Closing her eyes, Kendall sucked in a deep breath, held it, then exhaled slowly. "I don't want to lose Jonas, but I don't want to stay in this time."

"Then you'd better decide which means more to you."

"I know this is hard for you to understand," Kendall said sadly.

"But if you give up one, perhaps you'll find the other has no meaning. I don't think you can have both," Rose warned.

"Probably not," Kendall agreed, feeling that reality add a great weight to her already heavy heart.

Her spirits lifted somewhat when she heard the front door open. Jonas joined them in the dining room, carrying a small portfolio beneath his arm.

He greeted Rose, then came over and placed a kiss on Kendall's mouth that was neither brief nor perfunctory. It didn't end until Rose loudly cleared her throat.

"Sorry," Jonas said, though his light tone and bright smile indicated that he wasn't the least bit repentant for his behavior. "I think you'll be pleased," he said to Kendall as he untied the lacing and flipped open a collection of photographs from their wedding day.

"Wow," Kendall gushed as she turned the pages and recalled every minute of that day in minute detail.

"And I took the liberty of arranging for this," he said with flare as he presented her with a long box.

"What is it?"

"Open it and see," he said.

When she did, Kendall found a pendant, much more ornate than the one around her neck. Their initials had been carved on the cover, and when she flicked it open, she found her photograph on one side and Jonas's on the other.

"It's beautiful," she said as she held it out for him to attend to the clasp. "Take the other one off for now," she added in a smaller voice. It earned her a kiss on the neck that held great promise for the night ahead.

"YOU DIDN'T NEED to come with me," he said.

"I like Fairhaven," Kendall told him. "Besides, I'm not used to so much idle time."

"There's always needlework," he suggested with a playful wink.

"Lily Whitefield came by yesterday to suggest that I start sewing for the Confederate soldiers. She thought I would be a good candidate since I seemed 'adequate' with a needle and thread."

Jonas's laughter filled the carriage. "My scars are barely noticeable," he complimented. "And I understand many of our young Southern lads went north without sufficiently warm clothing."

"Don't get smug," Kendall warned. "The Union experiences several humiliating defeats at the hands of those Southern lads before the war turns."

"Care to tell me about any of them?"

"So you can pass that on? Sorry, Jonas. That's against the rules."

"It was worth a try," he said with a boyish grin that brought forth that incredible dimple. "After last night, I would have believed you incapable of denying me—"

His words were cut off by a sudden and loud explosion that sent their carriage tumbling to its side. Kendall cried out as she used her arms to try to soften the blow as she was bounced around the interior.

"Are you—"

Jonas was again silenced when the dirt just beyond the carriage erupted, spraying them with pebbles. Kendall felt the breath rush from her body as Jonas threw himself on top of her. The silence that followed was deafening, but somehow comforting. Apparently, whoever was firing the cannon believed they had hit their target.

"Are you all right?" Jonas asked.

"I will be when you get off of me," she managed to say.

Smiling apologetically, he rolled onto his side. At that instant, a large cannonball came crashing through the carriage, right toward Kendall's head.

Chapter Fourteen

"It's nothing," she told him for the third time.

"You're bleeding."

"It's just a scrape. I didn't even lose consciousness," she argued.

Jonas continued to part her hair and examine the abraised lump left when the cannonball had grazed the side of her head. Kendall sighed, thinking he had already done more than was necessary.

"Your leg must be killing you," she said, slapping him away from her. "Let me look at it. You shouldn't have carried me all the way here."

"I shouldn't have agreed to let you accompany me."

"Don't get macho on me," she pleaded. "And what is this place?"

"A hunting lodge," he explained. "We're at Fairhaven, just not anywhere near the house."

"Cozy," Kendall murmured dryly as she took in the collection of mounted and stuffed animals guarding the room. "Did you do all this?"

He shook his head. "Not all."

"I don't know whether to be glad or disgusted."

"By what?" he asked as he started a fire.

"I guess you don't hunt, you don't eat."

"Kendall," he breathed impatiently. "What are you going on about?"

"Gun control."

Shaking her head, she indicated that he should just forget it. That seemed to suit him, for he appeared quite distracted. And very, very tense. She watched as he prowled the room, checking each window in turn, his whole body coiled as if preparing to respond to some sensed danger.

"You're wound up tighter than a drum," she observed when she could no longer stand watching him flit from place to place. "Can the cannons from the blockade ships reach us here?"

"No."

"Then what is it?"

"I was guaranteed safe passage out here," he answered. "Something must be wrong."

Kendall got to her feet. "I thought you said we were riding out to Fairhaven because you needed to pick up supplies for the house?"

He didn't respond. He also didn't look at her.

"What are we really doing out here, Jonas?" she asked.

"The package I was supposed to receive last night was delayed. This is the alternative plan."

"We're spying?" she scoffed.

"I'm spying. You're just along because I couldn't think of a good reason to forbid it."

"How about the truth?" she asked. "Why didn't you tell me you had to do this?"

He turned then, meeting her eyes. "Would you have stayed behind?"

"No," she answered without hesitation. "I probably would have tried to talk you out of it."

He flashed her a boyish grin. "That was precisely my thought."

"You can't have all the benefits of marriage and just dismiss me when the mood strikes," she teased.

"Now you'll have to stay hidden when you hear a rider approach. I'm quite sure my compatriots will feel as Maitland does. Most of these men closely guard their identities along with their activities."

"And women," Kendall told him. "There are a few women in Richmond using their charms to get information from various military and government bigwigs."

"Care to share any names?"

"And get someone hanged?" Kendall asked innocently. "Sorry, but you'll have to fight your own battles."

"Is that why you examined Cecelia?" he asked as he kept his vigil at the window.

"I was hoping to find something to tell me the identity of the real killer."

"Then you still believe clearing my name is the key to getting back to your own time?"

"I'm trying to approach this logically," she told him.

"Is that why I saw you rubbing the locket in your hand and pretending you were talking to Rose?"

Kendall felt her cheeks grow warm. "Okay, so *now* I'm thinking logically. The locket belonged to Cecelia and she's dead. Your picture was inside, so you have to be the catalyst for all of this. I admired your picture, made some comment about wanting you, and wham-o."

"Back up," he said, finally giving her his full attention. "Explain the part about wanting me."

Kendall wished the rough pine flooring would open up and drop her into a deep hole. "I was having a conversation with Aunt Rose, and she was giving me a hard time about not dating. It was just a crack," she insisted, feeling herself blushing all the way to her toes. "I now have a new appreciation for the adage 'be careful what you wish for...'"

His dark head tilted slightly and he gave her a devastatingly sexy half smile. "You wished for me and...wham-o?"

"Pretty much," she admitted, trying to quell the desire budding in the pit of her stomach. When he looked at her like that, Kendall seemed able to forget that she didn't much like his century.

"Perhaps if I had the same thought, we could return together."

"That would be perfect, but finding yourself in a different time isn't a walk in the park."

Jonas left his sentry and came to her, lacing his fingers behind her waist and holding her against him. Kendall let her head fall back so that she could look into his eyes. What she saw there made her spirits soar.

"You're serious, aren't you? You would actually come with me if you could?"

"I would do anything to be with you, Kendall. Even if it means learning that a mouse is not only a creature but also an electronic assistant."

His head bent slowly and he was just about to kiss her, when the unmistakable sound of hoofbeats filtered through the cabin. Jonas gave her one of his "Why now?" looks and quickly shoved her into a spot hidden by the shadow of a large cabinet.

"You're late," Jonas said without preamble as soon as she heard the door open.

Kendall silently cursed the fact that she was hidden; it just grated on her natural curiosity. It also didn't explain why she suddenly smelled something vile, worse than an animal.

"Nice to see you again, Revell," a male voice answered. "What happened to your carriage?"

"We were fired upon."

"We?"

Kendall silently cringed.

"My driver and myself," Jonas answered. "He didn't make it."

She hadn't meant to, but hearing that the young houseman had died made her gasp. Immediately, she clamped her hand to her mouth, and didn't even dare breathe. Maybe no one had heard her.

"What was that?" there was definite suspicion behind the question.

"What?" Jonas asked.

She heard some sort of scuffle, then the unmistakable sound of fists meeting bodies. "Forget this," she grumbled as she pushed away from the wall. "Stop it!" she yelled when she found the two men crouched and poised for combat. There was a trickle of blood at the corner of Jonas's mouth. "He's half your size," Kendall continued as she went to her husband's side. "If you hit him, you'll probably kill him. Then how will that help your cause?"

"Who the blazes is she?"

Kendall turned to the young man and offered him her brightest smile. "I'm Kendall Revell," she said as she extended her hand.

Her overtly friendly actions seemed to confuse the man. He simply straightened and gawked at her.

"*This* is my wife," Jonas said from behind her.

Kendall almost winced when she heard the edge in his tone. There would no doubt be hell to pay later.

"She hasn't yet learned to obey," he whispered against her ear.

"This is your wife?"

"Careful, Preston," Jonas warned.

The young man finally smiled. The action gave him a warmth that seemed to counteract the almost rakish adventurousness she saw in his wild hair and disheveled clothing.

"My apologies, Lady Revell," he said as he bowed at the waist. Meeting Kendall's eyes, he added, "When I learned Jonas was being forced into yet another marriage, I envisioned some bovine-faced creature with a practical dowry. You," he began, taking her hand, "are a very pleasant surprise."

He brushed a kiss across her knuckles, and she could tell by the devilish twinkle in his eyes that the action was more to rankle Jonas than to impress her.

"You really shouldn't go around punching men twice your size," she said as she peered over her shoulder, to find Jonas scowling at them.

"You're as intelligent as you are beautiful," Preston commented.

"Will you please get your filthy hand off my wife?" Jonas said with obvious disdain. "What happened to you, anyway? You smell like..."

"A chicken coop?" he finished. "Afraid I was forced to hide last night when a Confederate soldier saw me riding toward town. Then I was forced to wait until the kindly farmer completed his chores before I could safely meet you here."

"What an adventure!" Kendall exclaimed.

"What an odor," Jonas complained. "Try not to touch anything while you're here."

"Jonas Revell! There must be a tub or basin in this place, and a change of clothes so that he can—"

"Oh, all right!" Jonas snapped. "I suppose we'll all be happier if young Preston bathes."

When the man was outside, she turned to her husband and spoke. "You didn't stick me behind that cabinet for my own safety," Kendall accused. "You just didn't want me to meet Preston. Why?"

Jonas shrugged. "I wasn't sure Preston would be the courier. If something had happened to him, it could have been anyone."

"Does your mouth hurt?" she asked.

"Yes," he answered, weaving his head when she attempted to touch his slightly bruised jaw. "I suppose you'll expect me to forget that he struck me?"

"He thought you had compromised him," Kendall stated. "You probably would have done the very same thing if your positions were reversed."

"I wouldn't have had to do anything if you had stayed home like a normal wife."

"But we both know I'm not a normal wife, don't we?" she said curtly, stung by his characterization.

"I didn't mean it like that," Jonas said, his voice soft and soothing. He wasted no time coming to her and wrapping her in his arms, gently stroking her hair as he placed a series of small kisses on the top of her head. "I only meant—"

"I do feel better!" Preston announced as he crashed through the door. "Sorry, didn't mean to interrupt."

"No one ever does," Jonas said with a sigh as he allowed her to step out of his embrace.

In addition to the damp towel, Preston had returned carrying his saddlebag on his shoulder. He hadn't bothered to fully button the overlarge shirt, and Kendall hoped that wasn't for her benefit—every man paled badly in comparison with Jonas.

"Make yourself presentable, man," Jonas instructed. "I can't have you offending my wife's sensibilities, now can I?'' Jonas gave her a private smile as he chastised the younger man.

''My apologies, Lady Revell,'' Preston said as he did his best to arrange the borrowed clothing. ''Mind if I cook up some eggs? I haven't eaten since yesterday.''

''I'll do it,'' Kendall offered as she watched him extract a dozen brown eggs from one of the compartments in his saddlebag.

''You will?'' Jonas asked, one dark brow arched in silent challenge.

Squaring her shoulders, she donned her most haughty posture. ''I can scramble eggs.''

''Of course you can,'' Jonas said with an I-don't-believe-it-for-a-minute smile. ''Please, get on with it.''

While the two men sat at the table discussing the likelihood of England and France offering assistance to the Confederacy, Kendall searched through the cabinets until she found what she needed. Breaking the eggs into the bowl and scrambling them went off without a hitch. It was only when she got to the actual cooking stage that she faltered.

There were some strange-looking iron things with wooden handles that seemed as if they might hold the pan over the fire, but how was she supposed to stir the eggs? And what was she supposed to use to keep the eggs from sticking to the incredibly heavy cast-iron skillet?

Grunting, she lifted the pan in both hands. It was only then that Jonas came to her aid. ''I'm afraid this lodge isn't equipped for use by a mere woman.''

She gave him a seething look. Preston's soft chuckle in the background didn't help, either. "Mere woman?" she repeated, highly affronted.

Jonas smiled at her. "Are you able to do this without assistance?" he taunted playfully. "You are welcome to try."

"I really hate it when you say that as if it were some sort of mantra," she teased back. "Now that I've done all the hard stuff, I'd be happy to let you do the rest."

"Stuff?" Preston asked when she joined him at the table.

"My wife has spent a good deal of time in the West. She has a whole host of unusual expressions."

"I've not made it west yet," Preston said conversationally. "Is it as wild and unspoiled as I've been told?"

"Parts of it," Kendall hedged. "Where are you from? I mean, I recognize your accent as British, but there's something else there, too."

"You've got a good ear. I was born in Shropshire, but my family came to America when I was a boy. We moved around a lot, depending on where Father could find work. Then I went to sea."

"You're a sailor?"

"That gives you two something in common," Jonas whispered when he brought a plate of steaming eggs over to the table.

"What?" Preston asked, obviously confused by Jonas's cryptic remark.

Smiling brightly, Kendall waited until Jonas had a mouthful of ale before she said, "He's referring to the fact that I curse like a sailor."

Crossing her arms, she simply sat back and allowed her husband to choke, cough and gasp all on his own. She also allowed him to clean up the mess he'd created.

"Jonas, you have truly found yourself a remarkable woman," Preston observed in the few seconds he stopped shoveling food into his mouth.

He certainly didn't have Jonas's refined mannerisms. Still, Kendall made an exception because of his ordeal. She'd been near a chicken coop once in her life, and she didn't look back on that experience with fondness.

"You'll have to get this to our Union contact before morning," Preston said. "And it can't go through Maitland because there's no money to pay his fees right now. This ship will sail from Liverpool in less than a month. We don't have time to wait to go through the normal channels."

"Before morning?" Jonas repeated as he unrolled the documents Preston had handed him. "That doesn't give me much time."

"I'd do it myself," Preston said, "but my ship is due to sail day after tomorrow at dawn. I have to get back to the Chesapeake Bay before I'm replaced. What with the war, commercial shipping is at a virtual standstill. It will be hard for me to reestablish my contacts if I don't sail with the *Mary Jane.*"

"I understand," Jonas said. "But I'll need you to ride to Fairhaven and have my groom send two mounts."

Preston's face contorted in a deep frown. "You're going to take her with you?"

Jonas made a sound. "No, I'm sending her back to town and I'll ride north." He turned his steely eyes on Kendall and added, "Alone."

The horses arrived within an hour of Preston's departure. It was quite dark, and Kendall didn't relish the thought of riding to Charleston alone at night.

"I have no sense of direction," she told him as soon as the groom had ridden off. "I'm not sure I can find my way. Couldn't I stay here?"

"No."

"Couldn't I stay at Fairhaven for the night?"

"Not when there's a whole garrison of antsy Confederate troops just a few miles on the other side of the Ashley River."

"But what if I get lost, or if I get stopped by a patrol?" she continued.

Jonas stopped fiddling with the strap of the saddle and let out a long sigh. "To be honest, I don't know what to do with you," he admitted.

"Take me with you," she answered.

"It isn't around the corner, Kendall. It will take hours of hard riding to get there."

"I can ride," she told him. "I might not be equestrian of the year, but I'd rather risk falling off that damned horse than roaming around here by myself."

"I shouldn't," he grumbled.

"Then I'll just follow you," Kendall promised him. "And before you tell me that I'm welcome to try, remember, I'm the one who never obeys."

"You have to be the most infuriating creature on earth," he said with a sigh as he bent down and cupped his hands in order for her to mount the horse.

"What is this?" she asked when she felt the lopsided padding beneath her fanny. "I can't ride sidesaddle, Jonas. I'll surely fall on my as—rear end."

"There's an old saddle in the lodge. Unstrap that one while I get it."

Kendall did as instructed, taking it one step further. It was a mistake. When she pulled the thing off the animal's back, she fell backward, with the saddle on top of her.

"I'm comforted to see you're such an accomplished horsewoman," Jonas said as he lifted the saddle off her. "It will be a pleasure having you along."

"There's no need for sarcasm," she told him. "I really won't slow you down. I'll even promise to be a good little wife."

He turned, his eyes glistening with surprise. "Does that mean you'll obey me?"

"This one time," she conceded. "And just until you've delivered whatever it is you're supposed to be delivering."

"Then it will be worth the trouble of having you along."

Kendall waited until he'd turned his back before she childishly offered him her tongue. When he had strapped on the new saddle, Kendall proudly hiked her skirts and mounted without his assistance.

"What you are doing is positively scandalous," he said, referring to the fact that she sat astride the horse, a great deal of thigh exposed for all to see.

"It's also immensely practical," she said as she grabbed the reins and followed him into the darkness.

When he had said several hours of hard riding, it wasn't an exaggeration. Every muscle in her body ached by the time they had delivered the documents and were nearly back to Charleston.

"Feeling all right?"

"Fine," she lied. She would have bitten off her tongue before ever admitting she should have taken his advice and gone back to the Rose Tattoo, regardless of her misgivings.

"I don't believe I have ever seen you this quiet. Are you sure you're not in any discomfort?"

The mocking tone, coupled with the fact that she was exhausted, ignited her fuse. "Okay. You were right. I don't have a muscle that isn't screaming bloody murder. My arms feel like lead and my butt is numb."

He threw his head back and laughed as he moved his horse abreast of hers. "Here," he said as he pulled up on her reins and brought both animals to an instant halt.

"What are you doing?"

"It's only about seven more miles to Charleston. We'll ride together so you can rest."

"Why didn't you make this offer about ten miles back?" Kendall grumbled as he lifted her, then settled her in front of him.

"I guess I was just enjoying your compliant behavior so much that I— Uumph!" he groaned as her elbow found his stomach. "The truth is, I didn't realize you were in such discomfort."

"I'm not now," she said as she rested her cheek against his shoulder and drank in the scent of him. "This reminds me of that first night," she mused. "It seems like forever ago now."

"Yes, it does."

"I was really mad that night. Especially when you had the audacity to tie me up."

"My mistake," Jonas answered easily as he gave her a gentle hug. "You should have told me that the best way to subdue you was to seduce you. It would have simplified things."

"That is so sexist," Kendall told him without any malice. "If you're coming back with me, you'll have to learn that you can't look at women as inferior objects good only to satisfy your carnal needs."

"As long as I have you, I won't need another woman to satisfy *anything*."

"You do know how to make a girl feel speci—"

Kendall's word was cut off when a gunshot rang out, causing her horse to bolt and Jonas's to rear. Another shot whooshed past her ear, close enough so that she could actually smell the hot metal.

Jonas dropped her to the ground as soon as he was able to get control of his animal. Then, without a word, he went tearing off in the direction of the next shot.

In the pale morning light, she couldn't see very far, and she wasn't sure whether it was better to go to the edge of the trees or race after Jonas. "I could never catch him," she mumbled. Lifting her skirt, she took refuge behind an oak tree and listened.

"Why did you have to go looking for trouble?" she whispered. The thought made her shake, and she gripped the rough surface of the tree, feeling scared and helpless. Those feelings intensified when she heard another shot. She waited for what seemed like an eternity, but it appeared that he wouldn't be coming back for her.

A vision of Jonas lying dead in the road brought tears to her eyes. Her head dropped as she allowed the tears to flow freely down her cheeks. "I never even actually told him I loved him," she spluttered. "I always made it part of my grand speeches about going home."

"Then I'll have to give you an opportunity to redeem yourself," Jonas said.

She looked up and blinked when she saw whom he had hog-tied over the front of his saddle.

Chapter Fifteen

"Harris Grisom was shooting at us?" she gasped.

"Probably not us, more likely me." He answered in a voice so laden with hatred that it actually made her shudder.

Jonas took his booted foot and rolled Harris off the horse. He fell at Kendall's feet, staring up at her with eyes filled with dread and animosity. A strip of fabric, obviously torn from his jacket, served as a gag, and his hands were bound with the same sort of rope Jonas had used to tie her all those weeks ago.

Jonas lowered himself to the ground and grabbed Harris by his tattered lapels. Hoisting him to his feet, he pulled another length of rope and attached Harris to the saddle horn.

"Is that really necessary?" Kendall asked.

"This horse can only accommodate two riders. He can walk, since his gunfire caused two perfectly good animals to run off."

Kendall shrugged, seeing his point. They rode slowly into town—Jonas apparently had no desire to cause

Harris pain. Their approach did, however, garner the attentions of nearly the entire city.

Kendall was amazed by the number of people who ran out on porches and front verandas to gawk at Harris Grisom being led up Bay Street. Yet no one, except Dylan Tanner, stepped forward.

"Jonas," Dylan said as he trotted up beside them. "What is going on?"

"You'll find out as soon as I do."

Dylan mumbled something she couldn't understand as he went forward and met them at the front of the Rose Tattoo.

Jonas dismounted from Grisom's horse, then lifted Kendall down before unlooping the rope from the saddle horn and tugging Harris up the front steps.

"Do you know what this is all about?" Dylan asked her as a very stunned Mrs. McCafferty opened the door.

"Not really," Kendall admitted.

"Where have the two of you been?"

"Out at Fairhaven," she answered.

"What is important," Jonas began as he yanked his prisoner into the parlor, "is that Grisom has made three attempts on my life, and in this last one, he very nearly killed Kendall."

Dylan's eyes grew wide as he looked at her. She saw his gaze travel to the lump on the side of her head.

Answering his thoughts, Kendall said, "That was another mishap. Luckily, Harris is a pretty bad shot."

The bound-and-gagged man began to mumble beneath the cloth stuffed in his mouth. Jonas responded by shoving him into a chair.

"I want him arrested and prosecuted," Jonas told Dylan. "I also want the charge to include the loss of one of my horses—a very valuable mare."

Dylan raked his fingers through his hair, his handsome features conveying his utter dismay at this strange turn of events.

Before they got much further, Rose and Shelby arrived. Apparently, word of the situation had brought them running.

Harris struggled against his restraints, but appeared to know better than to try to move from the spot where Jonas had shoved him.

"I appreciate that there's some bad blood between you two," Dylan began, "but dragging him through town probably wasn't such a good idea."

Jonas's expression was stonelike in its intensity. "I know the Confederate occupation of the city has seriously limited your powers, but even Monroe won't be able to overlook this." Jonas reached into the back of his waistband and produced a rather impressive handgun.

It was a large weapon with some sort of bleached bone carved into a handle. The sight of it instantly filled Kendall with misgiving, yet she couldn't figure out why. But there was something about seeing the gun that set off a warning light in her brain.

"How did you get that?" Dylan asked.

"I took it away from the bastard just before he fired his fourth shot."

Dylan looked at Kendall for affirmation. She nodded, then recapped what had happened when they were on the deserted roadway.

"What the hell were you doing out on the Columbia Highway at dawn?" Dylan asked.

"Retrieving my wife," Jonas answered as his eyes found her in the group.

"I'm afraid I went riding and lost my way," Kendall lied. "I never have had much of a sense of direction."

Dylan looked from Jonas to her, then shrugged, apparently not interested in challenging the lame story.

"Don't you think we should untie him?" Rose suggested as she pulled one of her cigarettes out and lit it, taking a long drag and blowing out a stream of blue smoke.

"I really should hear his side of it," Dylan said, eyeing Jonas.

Giving a curt nod, Jonas reached over and pulled the gag from Harris's mouth. The man immediately began to spit and sputter about Jonas being a murderer.

"I'll be happy to ram this back down your throat," Jonas warned.

The small man glared up at Jonas with unbridled hatred. "I only wanted see to it that you suffered for killing my Cecelia. Since the law hasn't been able to touch you, I was within my rights as a father."

"Really?" Jonas said, sounding almost bored. "Since you brought up fathers, want to tell me the name of the father of the baby Cecelia was carrying when you pawned her off on me?''

Harris went white, Shelby sucked in a breath, and Rose made a sound that wasn't really surprise, but more like the dawn of understanding.

"I don't know what you're talking about," Harris claimed.

"Cecelia was pregnant when she died," Kendall stated. Not so much for Harris's benefit, but because she knew the three other people in the room would heed her diagnosis. "You had to have known."

"What went wrong, Harris?" Jonas asked as he bent forward and spoke next to the man's ear, his voice filled with loathing. "You couldn't bribe her lover into marrying her, so you came to me because you knew I needed the wharf?"

"Yes," the red-faced man hissed. "I knew I could count on your greed to solve the problem. You've got just enough of that British practicality that I knew you'd be the perfect choice. I'm just surprised Cecelia told you."

"Harris?" Shelby asked as she came forward. "How could you convince your daughter to marry Jonas if you knew she was carrying another man's child? Surely she would have preferred to marry the man she was in love with."

"She wouldn't reveal his name!" Harris yelled. "I begged and pleaded with her, but she wouldn't tell me anything more than the fact that she had told him about the baby and he'd shunned her."

"That explains why she looked like a zombie when she married Jonas," Rose observed. "I always wondered why she had that vacant look in her eyes on what should have been the happiest day of her life."

"If what you're saying is true..." Kendall began, thinking aloud. She met Jonas's eyes. "Then it makes more sense that her lover killed her. He probably didn't want to risk Cecelia telling you the truth. If she knew Jonas at all, she would have known he wouldn't have taken her deception quietly."

"But Caroline was here," Harris reminded her. "She swears no one but Jonas was in the house that night. No one but him could have thrown her from that window."

"You managed to get upstairs without being seen," Kendall accused. "The first time you tried to kill Jonas."

"That wasn't me," Harris insisted, looking to Dylan. "I swear, I wasn't the one who shot at him the night he brought *her* here."

Jonas slapped him on the side of his head. "Careful how you address my wife, Grisom."

"But I'm telling the truth. This morning was the first opportunity I had to make things right."

Realization came to Kendall in a sudden flash. "It wasn't the same gun," she murmured.

"What?" Jonas asked.

"On the night you were shot, I saw the gun just before the person fired. It wasn't the same as that one," she explained, pointing to the gun Dylan now held. "I would have remembered that handle. The gun I saw that night was plain.''

"You mean there are *two* people intent on killing him?" Rose asked.

"Well, we have one of them right here," Jonas said as he yanked Harris to his feet. "And I'm taking this one directly to Monroe."

"But, Jonas, what if Monroe was the father of Cecelia's child?"

"Monroe?" Dylan, Rose and Harris all asked at the same instant.

"He did tell Kendall and I that he was in love with Cecelia," Shelby verified. "Is it possible that he's the person responsible for the other attempts on your life?" she asked Jonas.

Jonas nodded, but Kendall kept her reservations to herself. It was certainly a strong possibility. If Jonas was right and Monroe was totally devoted to his mother, he wouldn't want word of his callous treatment of Cecelia to become public. And he did seem overtly hostile toward Jonas.

"Let's go," Jonas said.

With Dylan in charge of the prisoner, Jonas and Kendall followed behind, walking arm and arm. "Once we have this settled, I promise you'll be able to get some rest," he said against her ear.

"I couldn't sleep while this keyed up," she told him. "Something about all of this doesn't feel right."

Jonas slowed their pace so that they were out of the earshot of Dylan and Harris. "Maybe because we're so close to finding the answer that will send you back to your time.''

She leaned against him, closing her eyes. "I'm going to hope we go together, Jonas. If I can travel through time, you should be able to do the same."

"And if I can't?" he asked with a heaviness to his words that she felt just as strongly.

"Let's not think about that now," she whispered.

They weren't exactly welcomed with open arms when they arrived at Monroe's office.

"What's the meaning of this, Tanner?" Monroe bellowed. "And why is that man bound?"

"He's under arrest for attempting to kill the Revells," Dylan answered as he deposited Harris in one of the chairs opposite Monroe's massive desk.

"I think you have it backward," Monroe argued. "Revell is the killer we've been after."

"You've been after," Kendall corrected. "And now we all understand why it was so important for you to arrest Jonas for your crime."

"My c-crime?" Monroe stammered. "I didn't kill Cecelia. I believe I explained why that was an absurdity," he added, leveling his gaze on Kendall.

"I know what you told me," she answered. "And I also know about the baby."

"Baby? What baby?"

Jonas took a threatening step toward the man. Resting his fingertips against the desk, he leaned forward, getting right into the other man's face. "It seems Cecelia was three months along on our wedding day. Care to shed any light on that?"

Monroe's face was so expressive that Kendall didn't think it was fake. In fact, the man seemed so genuinely stunned by the news that he collapsed into his chair with his jaw still dangling open. "Not Cecelia," he whispered. There was such worship, such reverence, behind the exclamation that Kendall was immediately convinced that Monroe was not the one responsible for Cecelia's pregnancy.

Jonas must have come to the same conclusion, for he stepped away from the desk and moved to her side.

"Even if you didn't know about the baby, that doesn't mean you can't be responsible for the attempt on Jonas's life," Dylan stated.

That seemed to bring the man out of his daze. "But I thought you just said you had evidence that Harris tried to kill Revell."

"I attacked him on the road," Harris admitted. "I couldn't stand the thought that he had killed my daughter and then refused to return her dowry."

"What about the stabbing?" Kendall pressed. "Was that you, as well?"

Harris Grisom appeared genuinely shocked by her question. "Of course not. I wouldn't be so stupid as to attempt to kill Jonas in a face-to-face confrontation. Look at his size!"

"Smart man," Jonas observed wryly. "Not a particularly accurate shot, but you were wise not to come after me."

"So who do you know that isn't so wise?" Kendall asked.

Jonas didn't answer with words, but his eyes indicated that he had an idea.

After leaving Dylan and Monroe to work out the details of Harris's arrest, Kendall and Jonas headed home.

"Maitland, right?" she guessed.

"He's the only one I can think of. And the shooting and stabbing did happen after I compromised his position by refusing to allow him to kill you."

"But I thought he needed you and vice versa."

Jonas shrugged. "He could always find someone to replace me. He knows most of my contacts. It might take him a bit longer to get information out of England, but he's a resourceful chap."

"So what are you going to do about it?"

"You don't want to know."

Kendall grabbed a handful of his shirtsleeve and tugged him to a halt. "While I agree that you're probably right about Maitland, what if you're wrong? Just like all that evidence pointing to Monroe, but he wasn't Cecelia's lover."

"So he said."

"C'mon, Jonas. He was absolutely devastated to hear that she was pregnant when she died. Obviously, he had her up on a pedestal, but he was definitely admiring her from afar."

"But Maitland isn't Monroe. He isn't afraid to kill."

Kendall shivered, recalling just how willing Maitland had been to do her in on that first night. "But killing you would put a definite crimp in his wallet. And you told me that he was so lacking in principle that he was selling out his own country just to make a fast dollar. But what if..."

Jonas shook his head. "If you're going to suggest that Maitland and Cecelia were lovers, I would have to take issue."

"Why?"

"Because Maitland would have married her. Especially with the added inducement of an interest in the wharf. Do you realize how much income comes from that wharf? It is the only route for more than fifty plantations to get their crops to Europe. The north has virtually choked off all other outlets. Without the money from selling our crops abroad, the Confederacy would go bankrupt inside of a week."

"But I heard what Maitland said to you," Kendall reminded him. "He was almost laughing when he spoke of Cecelia's murder and how convenient it was. Perhaps he wasn't just talking about your spying activities."

"So now you're saying that you don't think Maitland tried to kill me, but you do think he killed Cecelia?"

She stiffened when she heard the mocking tone in his voice. "It's a possibility," she told him. "*Someone* pushed that girl out of the window."

"I know, Kendall. I found her body."

"Tell me *exactly* what you found."

Jonas grunted in disgust as they climbed the front steps to the house. "Not now, Kendall. I'm tired and I just want to get some rest."

"But it could help me learn more about what might have happened. If I can get the trajectory of the body, I can calculate the probable height of the assailant."

"Kendall," he warned. "Haven't we had enough excitement for one day?"

"Apparently not," she answered when the door was opened by a tearful Caroline Grisom.

Chapter Sixteen

"Not now, Caroline," Jonas said as he brushed past the girl, keeping his hand at Kendall's waist.

"I tried to get her to leave," Mrs. McCafferty announced with definite irritation in her brogue. "I told her right where she could find that despicable father of hers."

Caroline burst into a chorus of gut-wrenching sobs, and Jonas looked at the ceiling, wondering what he was going to do with this pathetic creature. After years of being trained not to ignore a woman in distress, Jonas sighed and looked pleadingly at Kendall.

"Let's hear what she has to say."

He gave her a grateful smile before ushering the sobbing girl into the dining room and suggesting that Mrs. McCafferty make some tea.

"Please don't have my father charged, Jonas. I couldn't stand it if he went to prison. He's all I have."

"You didn't seem to mind if Jonas went to prison," he heard Kendall retort.

There was a definite possessiveness to her tone that warmed him. It was obvious from her stiff posture as she sat near Caroline that Kendall's desire to protect him was as strong as the other desires he had discovered during their time together. Perhaps that was a sign that she would stay.

"I only said what I did to help my father." Caroline hiccuped. "I thought if you believed Jonas was guilty, you would want to get him away from here to keep him from being hanged."

"I might have, if I'd believed you," Kendall answered.

"Why is it so important to you that I leave?" Jonas asked, feeling his patience nearing an end after being reminded of her accusations.

"You must return your interest in the wharf to Father. It's his only hope."

"He won't need money where he's going," Jonas observed. Of course that observation did nothing but send Caroline into yet another fit of tears.

Kendall gave him a private look that fairly pleaded for compassion. He wondered where her capacity for kindness came from, given the fact that Caroline and her family had been the cause of so much of their difficulties.

"Why is the wharf so important?" Kendall asked. "Surely your father has sufficient income to live comfortably from his share."

"It isn't his," Caroline admitted in a voice so soft it was barely audible. "It belongs to William Whitefield."

"What are you talking about?" Jonas asked, obviously exasperated. "Your father has owned that property for years."

Caroline folded her hands in her lap and fixed her eyes on them. Her shoulders still shook with an occasional sniff.

"Caroline," Kendall began calmly. "If you expect Jonas to help you, you'll have to give him good reason."

"Father has had a problem for some time," Caroline answered carefully.

"If you're talking about his gambling, I know all about it," Jonas said. "Anyone who has ever been inside the Palace knows of your father's passion for cards."

"The Palace?" Kendall asked, looking up to meet his eyes.

Jonas swallowed hard and said, "It's a club for gentlemen."

"And what sort of things do gentlemen do at this club?" she challenged.

Jonas felt his face grow warm. "Exactly what you think they do."

"Is this an establishment you have frequented in the past?"

Jonas went over and placed his hand on her shoulder, "Not in recent history," he assured her.

Kendall drew her eyes away from Jonas's and turned back to Caroline. "So your father owes money?"

Caroline shook her head. "Not money. He signed a note for the wharf."

"When did he do this?" Jonas asked.

"Just after Cecelia died. He thought you would do the honorable thing and refuse to accept her dowry in light of her death."

"I might have, if you and your family hadn't been so quick to accuse me of killing her."

"I know you didn't kill my sister," Caroline said.

"But because of the things you've said to Kendall— and Lord knows who else—no one in this town will ever believe otherwise."

Caroline shifted uneasily in her chair. "I'm sorry, Jonas. Truly I am. I swear, if you'll just refuse to press charges, I promise I won't ever make that accusation again."

"That's all well and good," Kendall said. "But it won't undo the damage that has already been done. And who's to say your father won't get out of jail and come gunning for Jonas again."

"I'll talk to him," Caroline answered. "I'll even move back to the house to keep an eye on him."

"You're awfully quiet," Kendall observed when they were alone in their room. They had left Mrs. McCafferty to see to Caroline, suggesting the girl nap to regain her composure while she and Jonas weighed their options.

"I'm thinking," Jonas said.

"I'm thinking, too," Kendall told him as she sat at the dressing table, toying with Cecelia's locket. "Tell me where you found her body, Jonas."

"Must I?" he asked.

She could hear the wariness in his voice. "Humor me," she said as she flicked open the locket and compared the picture with the man lying on the bed. "It could be important."

"I found her directly below the window."

"How directly?" Kendall pressed.

"Maybe a foot or so out from the building."

"Get up," she told him excitedly.

"I'm tired, Kendall. I—"

"We have to talk to Caroline again," she insisted, going over to give his arm a pull.

Reluctantly, Jonas hoisted himself off the bed and followed her across the hall.

Kendall didn't bother to knock. She simply opened the door and found Caroline in a chair, clutching her small purse in her lap. She looked up at them with wide, frightened eyes.

"Who was the father of Cecelia's baby?" Kendall asked even before she stopped walking.

"I—I don't know what you're talking about," Caroline stammered. "What baby?"

"Don't lie to me," Kendall warned. "Cecelia had to confide in someone. I'm betting it was you."

"You're mistaken," Caroline said as she lowered her eyes. "I don't know where you got such an idea. Cecelia and Jonas were only married a matter of hours."

"Fine," Kendall said on a breath. "Then your father can spend the rest of his life in jail."

Turning on the balls of her feet, she grasped Jonas's hand and began to pull him from the room.

"Wait!" Caroline called.

Kendall gave Jonas an encouraging smile before she turned to face the reluctant young girl. "You know the identity of the man. Tell me and we'll have him arrested for trying to kill Jonas on the first two occasions. So long as Jonas agrees, the charges against your father will be dropped."

"They will?" Jonas asked, obviously skeptical.

She turned, faced her husband and said, "Bigger fish, Jonas. Harris was acting on his grief. Surely you can make allowances for that."

"Don't be so sure," he grumbled.

"Well, Caroline, which will it be? Your father, or the identity of the baby's father?"

Caroline pulled her lower lip between her teeth and thought for a few seconds. "William Whitefield. He and Cecelia were lovers."

"I guess we know who killed Cecelia now," Jonas said.

There was no relief, no gladness, no emotion in that statement, and Kendall knew the reason.

"We don't," Kendall told him. "But Caroline does, don't you?"

The girl shifted uncomfortably in her seat. "I suppose it could have been Captain Whitefield. Cecelia said he had laughed when she told him about the baby. She said he had no intention of marrying her. Apparently, he had more important plans for his future than being married to the daughter of a merchant."

"Caroline," Kendall began sternly. "Stop lying. We both know that Captain Whitefield might be guilty of treating your sister horribly, but he didn't kill her."

"You?" Jonas said from behind her, his eyes wide as he looked upon Caroline with total shock. "You killed your own sister?"

Caroline began to sob again, tears streaming down her cheeks.

"I don't believe this," Jonas growled. "All this time and she's the one who—"

"You aren't seeing the forest for the trees," Kendall told him. Turning her back on the tearful Caroline, she moved to stand in front of Jonas. Taking his hands in hers, she lifted her chin to meet his bewildered gray eyes. The smile she offered held a mixture of sadness and apology. "Don't you get it, Jonas?"

"Get what? She was the only other person in the house."

"No," she said with profound sorrow. "There was one other person in the house. A person who was apparently unable to cope with the idea of living."

She watched as the meaning of her words registered in his expression. "You think she killed herself?"

Kendall nodded once, then turned to Caroline. "You've known that all along, haven't you?"

Caroline's head bobbed as she continued to cry.

"How did you figure this out?"

Kendall turned her attention back to her husband and said, "When you told me where you had found her. If she'd been thrown, she would have landed a greater distance from the building."

"I see," Jonas said softly. "Why didn't she just tell me she couldn't tolerate the idea of being married to me?" he asked.

"Caroline," Kendall began softly as she went over to the girl. "Letting Jonas believe that he's the reason your sister killed herself is just as wrong as telling people he killed her. Please, give him the note."

"How did you know?" Caroline whispered.

"I guessed. You told too many lies and they caught up with you. But you can change all that now."

"But if word gets out that Cecelia killed herself, she'll be branded a sinner."

"No one beyond the family needs to know," Kendall assured her. "It's either the note, or your father goes to jail for a very long time and Whitefield goes unpunished."

"Do you feel better?" Kendall asked, disapproval dripping from each word.

"Yes," he told her, trying not to stare at the locket around her neck. It wasn't the locket he'd had made specifically for her; it was Cecelia's locket. "When I learned Whitefield had only seduced Cecelia to get close to her father, just so he could get into his card game, I felt like slapping him. When he finally admitted that he only wanted control of the wharf to refuse my stores and put Fairhaven into bankruptcy, I felt like strangling him. Punching him was actually an act of kindness."

"I know I would have done the same thing," Rose piped in. "Whitefield deserved it, but I think you're a fool for letting Grisom go free."

"Now, Rose," Shelby cautioned. "That really was Jonas's decision, and it isn't as if the man hasn't suffered a great deal already."

"He tried to kill them," Rose snorted. "Tell her, Dylan."

"I'm afraid I can see Shelby's point. I was at the jail when Caroline came in and spoke to her father. Whatever she told Grisom had a profound effect on him. When I released him, he seemed to be off in another world."

"Which is where you're planning on going, right?" Jonas said so only Kendall could hear.

"Not until I've had a chance to say goodbye," she told him. "And don't look so crestfallen. I've proved your innocence and I'm still here, so I could be on the wrong track and you're going to be stuck with me for the duration."

Jonas had to admit, the idea held definite appeal.

"So how do you plan on going back to your time?" Shelby asked.

"With your help."

Rose stiffened and Shelby looked afraid.

"Don't worry. I'm not going to ask you to do anything other than help me recreate the afternoon that it happened."

"And if that doesn't work?" Jonas asked.

He saw the flash of sadness cross her eyes in spite of the bright smile she offered. "I'll stay here, I guess."

At Kendall's direction, they waited until the exact time she had gone to have that fateful lunch with her aunt. She gave Shelby and Rose their dialogue, which left Jonas and Dylan nothing to do but to stand back and observe.

"I guess it will be hard watching her disappear into thin air," Dylan said.

"'Hard' doesn't even begin to describe it," he admitted. Jonas reached into his pocket and pulled out the pendant that he had given Kendall. Opening it, he stared at her picture and wondered if she would even remember him once she got back to her own time.

"Okay," Kendall said. "I slipped the picture of Jonas back in the—"

"Wait!" he called out.

Jonas went to her, gathered her into his arms and kissed her hard. When he set her down, he looked into her eyes, silently praying that she wouldn't leave, knowing he loved her too much to insist that she stay.

"I love you, Kendall," he said on a voice choked with raw emotion.

"I love you, too," she told him. "I always will."

All he could focus on as he gazed down into those blue eyes that were shimmering with tears was how he didn't think he could continue living without her. He genuinely understood what had driven Cecelia to madness.

"I know this is against the rules, but I'd like to ask a favor."

"Anything," she whispered as she brought her hand up to rest on his cheek.

Jonas opened the locket and took out the miniature photograph of Kendall in her wedding dress. "I want you to remember me, Kendall. I want you to remember everything we shared."

"I will, Jonas. It's all here," she said, placing her hand over her heart.

"Take this with you," he said as he lifted Cecelia's locket. "When you're back where you belong, maybe this will remind you that I'll never love or want anyone the way I've loved and wanted you."

Jonas slipped the picture into the empty space, placed it over her head, and as he did, he experienced a flash of bright light.

Chapter Seventeen

"First you disappear—now you've spent nearly a week moping around like the dead!" Rose complained.

"Leave me alone," Kendall groaned as she pulled the covers over her head. "And give me back the key to my apartment. I told you yesterday I didn't feel like company."

"I know what you told me," Rose said as she yanked the bedspread, as well as the sheets off the bed. "I'm just trying to figure out what's gotten into you. You look like hell."

"Thank you," Kendall retorted smartly. "Now that you've stated the obvious, why don't you leave?"

"Because I'm not going to sit by and let you destroy your life."

"I already have," Kendall murmured, fighting back tears.

"I talked to Joan today, and she said you only had one more week of comp time left. If you don't go back to the hospital by Monday, they'll fire you."

"So?"

"Kendall Butler!" Rose yelled as she placed her hands on her hips. "You worked too long and too hard to become a doctor to take this attitude now. Tell me what the hell is wrong and maybe I can help."

Kendall shook her head as she absently rubbed her locket between her fingers. "Everything is wrong. And it isn't something you can fix."

"If you won't talk to me, will you talk to Shelby? She's as worried about you as I am."

"Please, Aunt Rose. Don't send in reinforcements. I just need some time to myself."

"You've had weeks of time," Rose countered stubbornly. "And where the hell were you that you couldn't even pick up the phone?"

"I've already told you—I wasn't someplace where they had phones."

"Kendall, honey," Rose began as she sat on the edge of the bed. "I'll back off if you don't want to tell me what's wrong, but you've got to get out of this apartment and back among the living."

"I will," she hedged.

"When?"

"When I feel like it."

"Not good enough," Rose announced. "We're having a private party for Shelby's birthday tomorrow night after closing. If you aren't there by eleven-thirty, I swear I will come over here and drag you out of here myself."

"I don't feel like a party."

"I don't really care," Rose answered angrily. "There's nothing uglier than a person drowning herself in self-pity. Shelby has been a good friend to you.

The least you can do is come and wish her a happy birthday.''

"Fine," Kendall said, relenting. "But that's all I'm willing to do.''

"What about your job? Are you going to let them fire you?''

"Aunt Rose," Kendall warned as she met the steely green eyes. "I said I would come to the party. I haven't decided what I'm going to do about work yet, but when I do, I promise I'll let you know.''

"You're as pigheaded as your father was," Rose mumbled.

"Did my father have an accident when he was a child?" Kendall asked.

Rose's brows drew together before she answered. "I haven't thought about that in years," she mused. "Raymond was riding his bike and I challenged him to race me down a big hill. He lost control of his bike and was almost killed. He was about five. Why?''

"Just boning up on the family tree," Kendall answered. "Were you named after someone? I mean, some relative?''

Rose shrugged. "I think so, but I'd have to dig out the family Bible to find out who. I've never placed much stock in that sort of thing. Live for the present," she said, wagging her finger at Kendall. "Why this sudden interest in genealogy?''

Kendall shrugged. "It's something to do."

"What you need to do is take a shower, get out of this apartment and get over whatever it is that's put you in such a foul mood.''

Kendall sighed, holding the locket more tightly.

"Was it a man?" Rose asked. "Is that what this is all about?"

"Why would you think that?" Kendall answered, not meeting her aunt's eyes. "We both know I haven't had much luck in that department."

"Unless you met someone on your mystery vacation."

Apparently, Kendall's silence was all the confirmation Rose needed. "If that's the case, I know the perfect solution. When you have a bad experience with a man, you don't mope—you find a replacement."

"Is that why you never dated anyone after Uncle Joe left?"

"We aren't discussing me," Rose snapped. "And besides, it seems your uncle has finally come to his senses."

"What?"

Rose actually blushed. "We've seen each other a couple of times since he came back from Florida."

Rose said it as if her ex-husband had been away at Disney World instead of spending the past twenty years married to someone else.

"Good for you."

"Is there any possibility you could get a second chance with your man?" Rose asked.

"Nope," Kendall answered.

"Is he married?"

Thinking of the gold band in the drawer of her nightstand, Kendall simply nodded.

"Then you're well rid of him," Rose insisted. "I thought you would have been smarter than to get yourself involved with a married man."

"Me, too."

WHETHER IT WAS because she feared another scene with her aunt or the fact that some of Rose's words had penetrated her brain, Kendall wasn't entirely sure. Since she had suddenly reappeared in her apartment, she wasn't sure of much of anything other than how much she missed Jonas. Whatever the reason, she had actually taken a shower, fixed her hair and applied a small amount of makeup before slipping on a simple black dress made of a clingy material. It wasn't her usual style, but if she was going to get her aunt off her back, she needed to look the part. The display of spandex was sure to keep Rose at bay for a while.

She had also called the chief of her department and smoothed things over so that she could return to work the following Monday. Now her only problem was the nagging fatigue and slight flu that had plagued her ever since her return from the past.

"Probably some sort of time-travel jet lag," she grumbled as she stepped into her heels. After running a brush through her hair, she slipped her locket over her head and added a pair of silver earrings. She looked okay, unless anyone bothered to peer into her eyes. They were dull and lifeless. But she forced that thought to the back of her mind. Just as she kept trying to keep the memory of Jonas locked there.

She parked her car at the rear of the Rose Tattoo, under the sign marked Employees Only. There were only a few other cars in the lot and she recognized all but one. She smiled, thinking the car must surely belong to whomever Rose had hired to replace the clumsy waiter she'd encountered on her last visit.

She stood outside for a minute, remembering vividly what the place had looked like when it had been her home. "Not a healthy thought. Just pretend it never happened," she told herself as she pushed open the kitchen door.

"Hi, Kendall," Susan said. "They're all in the dining room. Boy, is your karma ever screwed up."

"Thanks," Kendall replied. "I knew that already."

"You should probably see someone about that," the girl continued as she placed a number of candles atop a beautifully decorated cake. "I know a good—"

"Thanks all the same," Kendall interrupted.

"There you are," Rose said as she came through the swinging metal door that led to the dining area. "I was afraid I was going to have to come for you. Good, you look wonderful."

"I tried," Kendall remarked, plastering a smile on her face.

"Listen," Rose began as she took Kendall's arm and led her toward the stairway. "I've got a small surprise for you."

Kendall took one look at her aunt's face and started up the stairs. "How could you?" she asked. "Whoever he is, get rid of him. I'll wait in the office until he's long gone."

"Be reasonable, Kendall," Rose argued. "He's a great guy and really nice looking. And he says—"

"I don't care if he's God's gift to women. If he says so much as hello to me, I'll blow him away."

"You're welcome to try."

Kendall made a noise as she turned toward the familiar voice. "Jonas?"

"Wait a minute, you two *do* know each other?" Rose asked.

"Yes," they answered in unison.

"Leave us alone, Aunt Rose," Kendall stated as if in a trance.

"But the party?"

"We'll be down in a minute," Kendall said as she finally came out of her daze and climbed the stairs two at a time to throw herself into his arms.

"I guess you do know each other," she heard Rose say smugly when their mouths joined in a hungry kiss.

"What happened?" she asked when she eventually had a chance to drag him into the office.

"I'm not sure, but I ended up out in the middle of some field. I wandered around for two days and then I got arrested."

"What?"

He smiled almost shyly. "I tried to explain to the police officer that I was from 1861 and had followed my wife through time."

"You didn't."

"It gave me a better understanding of how you must have felt when none of us would believe you."

"Frustrating, huh?" she asked as she ran her hands over his chest. "I like you in contemporary clothing. Who took you shopping?"

"Dylan."

"You didn't tell him?"

Jonas was shaking his head from side to side almost violently. "When they told me I was free to go after my forty-eight hours of observation, I came here, hoping to find you."

"You must have looked cute roaming the streets in your period costume," she teased.

"I did get some rather interesting reactions."

"How did you find Dylan?"

Jonas lifted a lock of her hair as he answered. "He found me. I was hanging around out back and I guess I scared Shelby or something. The next thing I knew, he was on top of me."

"Dylan doesn't take kindly to having his wife threatened."

"I wasn't threatening her. I was waiting for you."

"And you told Dylan that?"

"He didn't believe me, though. He would have taken me back to that awful diagnostic center again if Rose hadn't shown up."

"When was that?"

"Yesterday."

"And you didn't call me?"

He shook his head. "Rose wouldn't allow it. She said if I was lying, she'd ring my neck and then call my wife. Know anything about that?"

Kendall smiled up at him. "I did tell her I had met a man, but that he was married."

"You failed to tell her I was married to you, I take it?"

"I guess I did."

"Then I think you need some reminding, Lady Revell," he said as he swept the contents on Rose's desk to the floor and laid her on the surface. He wasted no time settling on top of her, their lips locked in a passionate kiss. Her hands touched him every place she could reach, while she marveled in the feel of his magical mouth.

She ran her hands over his back, feeling his strength beneath the softness of his shirt. A fire began to smolder in the very core of her being and she surrendered to it completely.

Until Dylan and Rose came bursting into the room.

"Kendall Butler, what on earth do you think you're doing?"

Her smile must have looked as guilty as she felt. "I guess we just forgot where we were."

Rose's frown wasn't quite as fierce as it could have been. "You made one hell of a mess of my things," she said, eyeing the scattered papers. "And couldn't this have waited until you got home?"

"I am ho—"

"What Jonas means," Kendall interrupted, "is that I wasn't totally honest when I told you he was married."

Rose seemed visibly relieved. "Thank God. I would hate to think you two were carrying on like that if he was."

"He *is* married," she continued. "To me."

"I APOLOGIZE for anything and everything I ever said or thought when you were in my time," Jonas said as he showered her with kisses, not caring that he was causing some eyebrows to raise at the long table they were seated at. "When I was on my way here, I could have sworn I saw the man who worked at the livery . . . back when there was a livery on the corner."

Kendall laughed. "I think you'll find having a car dealership much more useful," she teased. "I can't believe you're actually, really, honestly here. In the flesh!"

"I can't, either," he admitted, looking suddenly quite serious. "What do you think hap—"

Kendall lifted her finger to his lips to quiet him. "Don't ask, Jonas. There are no answers. I only know that it doesn't make sense, but that I don't care because we're together again."

"But there has to be an explanation," he persisted. "Your Aunt Rose is the same woman I've known for years."

"Just chalk it up to magic, Jonas." She kissed him deeply. "At least I won't have to worry about your reaction to my aunt. She does have a habit of putting people off."

"One thing's for sure. I've never known Rose to be rendered speechless before," Jonas said.

"It *was* something of a new experience," Kendall admitted. She felt giddy as she played with the slice of cake on her plate. "Speaking of which—" she lowered her voice and placed her lips next to his ear "—have you suffered any ill effects since you got here?"

"Other than being arrested and being treated like a lunatic?"

"Yes," she giggled, knowing the feelings well.

"No, why?"

"No tiredness, no nausea?"

"Nope."

"Then it's probably a good thing you showed up."

"Why?"

"I'll tell you later. Some things a wife should tell her husband in private."

* * * * *

Turn the page for a bonus look at what's in
store for you in the next ROSE TATTOO.
It's a sneak preview of:

THE SILENT GROOM
by Kelsey Roberts
March 1997

The Silent Groom

"I cannot believe that you actually hired the first attorney you found in the phone book," Shelby groaned as she placed her hand on Rose's slumped shoulder.

"She wasn't the first. I made it all the way to the *B*'s." Her friend and business partner attempted a smile, though a night in jail dulled her expression. Shelby, along with everyone else at the Rose Tattoo, was terribly worried. In almost four years, she had never seen Rose Porter so upset.

Rose patted the rather lopsided mass of her hair with a nervous hand. "I won't have J.D. shelling out any more money on my account," she announced; her ferocious pride hung on each word. "Having to call my son to wire the bail money is about all the charity I can stand."

Shelby moved over behind the bar and poured two mugs of fresh coffee. Through the mirror behind the neatly aligned bottles of liquor, she could see Rose tilt back her head and close her eyes.

"I'm sure you can meet this woman tomorrow," Shelby suggested as she returned to the table. "By then

I'll have enough time to finish filling Gabriel in on what's happened.''

Rose's green eyes flew open, then narrowed. "I thought I said I didn't want you to do that. I can't afford to pay Mr. Langston, too. I'll bet private detectives are expensive as hell."

Shelby shrugged. "Dylan can't personally help you on this," she explained. "And Gabe has been nothing but gracious and friendly ever since he moved in across the street. Besides, he spends so much time here, he's probably desperate for the work. He doesn't seem to have any clients yet."

"How am I supposed to pay Langston *and* an attorney?" Rose fairly shouted. Strain was evident in her tense features. "I still haven't finished paying off my loan to Mitch Fallon.'

Reaching across the smooth surface of the table, Shelby covered Rose's hand with her own. She felt a small tremor. "Don't worry about the money, Rose. Your future is more important than money."

"But I didn't do it. When the police and that jackass of a prosecutor finally figure that out, I'll be buried beneath so much debt I'll probably have to sell my interest in this place."

"We need to focus on getting you out of this. We'll worry about the money later."

Rose snorted. "That's easy for you to say. You aren't the one writing the checks."

"But I would," Shelby said quietly. "You were there for me when Chad was kidnapped. I asked Gabe to help you. I'll make sure he's paid for his services."

"I don't like charity," Rose warned, her chin thrust out proudly. "I'm already into my son for a hundred thousand, and I have to give this woman a check when she gets here."

"Maybe you should talk to her first," Shelby said. "See if you think she's the right one to defend you. I've never heard of Joanna Boudreaux. I still think you ought to take J.D.'s suggestion and hire someone with—"

"I have already heard this from both my sons," Rose interrupted. "I'm sure she'll do just fine. Why should I pay some high-priced name when I'm innocent? Nothing but a foolish waste of money," she concluded as she rolled her head around on her shoulders. "Money I don't have."

"You know Wesley and J.D. will do anything for you, Rose. And neither would expect you to repay him."

Rose sat forward and leveled her green eyes on Shelby. "How can I ask them for help when the state of South Carolina claims I just murdered their father?"

HARLEQUIN®

I N T R I G U E®

THAT'S INTRIGUE—DYNAMIC ROMANCE AT ITS BEST!

Harlequin Intrigue is now bringing you more—more men and mystery, more desire and danger. If you've been looking for thrilling tales of contemporary passion and sensuous love stories with taut, edge-of-the-seat suspense—then you'll *love* Harlequin Intrigue!

Every month, you'll meet four new heroes who are guaranteed to make your spine tingle and your pulse pound. With them you'll enter into the exciting world of Harlequin Intrigue—where your life is on the line and so is your heart!

Harlequin Intrigue—we'll leave you breathless!

INT-GEN

Weddings by DeWilde

Since the turn of the century the elegant and fashionable
DeWilde stores have helped brides around the world
turn the fantasy of their "Special Day" into reality. But now the
store and three generations of family are torn apart by the
separation of Grace and Jeffrey DeWilde. Family members
face new challenges and loves in this fast-paced, glamorous,
internationally set series. For weddings and romance, glamour
and fun-filled entertainment, enter the world of DeWilde…

Watch for *FAMILY SECRETS*,
by Margaret St. George
Coming to you in December 1996

In an attempt to shed the past and get on with her future,
Grace DeWilde has left her new store and her new life in
San Francisco to return to England. Her trip results in a
devastating discovery about the DeWilde family that has
shocking implications for her children, for Ian Stanley,
whose unrequited love for Grace has been years in the
making, and for Jeffrey DeWilde, the estranged
husband Grace can never stop loving.

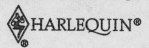

HARLEQUIN®

1997
Reader's Engagement Book
A calendar of important dates
and anniversaries for readers to use!

Informative and entertaining—with notable
dates and trivia highlighted throughout the year.

Handy, convenient, pocketbook size to help you
keep track of your own personal important dates.

Added bonus—contains $5.00 worth of coupons
for upcoming Harlequin and Silhouette books.
This calendar more than pays for itself!

Available beginning in November at
your favorite retail outlet.

HARLEQUIN®

Scandals

A passionate story of romance, where bold, daring characters set out to defy their world of propriety and strict social codes.

"Scandals—a story that will make your heart race and your pulse pound. Spectacular!"
—Suzanne Forster

"Devon is daring, dangerous and altogether delicious."
—Amanda Quick

Don't miss this wonderful full-length novel from Regency favorite Georgina Devon.

Available in December, wherever Harlequin books are sold.